Your

BAE IS

MY MAN

A Twisted Love Affair

LaSalle R.

Dedications

I want to tell my little cousin, LaDawn McAlister, happy birthday! We have always been close and you have always been more like a sister than a cousin. This book is for you and remember no matter what we go through you will forever mean the world to me.

-Your little, big cousin

Synopsis

In "Your Bae is My Man: A Twisted Love Affair," you'll meet Ember and Markus Ballard. On top of the world in every other aspect, the outside world can't tell that their empire is literally crumbling to the ground. When her husband's infidelities are exposed and she's forced to face the truth, Ember turns into the woman she swore she'd never be. When she discovers that he'll likely never change, will Ember dip out before it's too late? Or will she lose everything as she tries to fight for her marriage?

Prologue

I can't wait to have a weekend to spend quality time with the love of my life. This has to be the best weekend ever considering we both need a breather from the long hours at work. I can feel the strain the neglect is having on our marriage, and I can only imagine what it's doing to him. Lord knows I love this man with everything in me and there is nothing I wouldn't do for him. Just the thought of being able to see the smile on his face makes me smile from my soul. I don't know or understand the hold that man has on me, but I'm glad he does.

By trying to make this a weekend to remember, I call up my best friend to help me come up with something to fill the time with. Mya is my girl, and she may not be the most romantic, but she has been with her man for the last seven years. The only difference is Markus and I got married at the end of our first year together, whereas Mya and Lance have just stuck with being longtime boyfriend and girlfriend. I don't know if that's her doing or if it's something he wants.

The sound of her voice coming through the other end of the line pulls me back from my thoughts. "Em, what's up? Can you hear me?'

"Yeah, girl I just got lost in La La land. I need your help with something important," I start to explain.

"Hold up wait, wait, wait. If it has something to do with me putting on a dress forget it," she interrupts.

I don't know what the hell her problem is with dresses nowadays but this isn't the best friend I have known since high school. In the past, you couldn't beat her by putting on a dress to show off her curves. I guess that's just it, all that shit is in the past and there is no reason to keep reliving it and trying to make the present replay those memories.

"No, it's nothing that has to do with you getting dolled up. Even though it wouldn't hurt for you to get dressed up now and then. I mean you would look decent," I joked. "Seriously though I need your help with planning this weekend with Markus. We haven't had a weekend off together in a long time, and I took off this weekend because I knew he was going to be off. I need to make this something to make him smile. It has been hard for the both of us lately."

"I know. I'm the one you vent to all the time remember? So what did you have in mind or let's say what kind of weekend are we going for? You want a weekend that will end in you being pregnant or just something for the both of you to relax and be together?"

"Would it be fucked up if I said both?" I brace myself for her reaction. "I want to spend time with my baby. Hell, I miss his ass."

"Alright, I got you. Have you planned what you are going to have for dinner?"

"I haven't done anything. I was thinking about actually going to the black and white party they are having that Saturday. I need a day to get fine and show off my arm candy."

"You know damn well your arm candy will have fit in the middle of the damn party if his arm candy gets too much attention. So don't get too fine, but that's a good start. Now you are either going to have to cook or order takeout for dinner and make it a candlelight dinner. Run a hot bubble bath and pull him into it with you and rock his world."

"Ok now, what about before that? How should we spend the day?"

"I don't know. I'm making this up as I go."

"I know we should go to the gym together or have a spa day and massage one another all day, and I can take advantage of his nakedness. What do you think?"

"I think that's a good idea, and I can hear the smile growing wider and wider across your face."

I don't know what it is about that man, but there is nothing I love more than making love to him. Feeling his hands all over my body send tingles all over begging for him to keep them going, the sound of his breath in my ear as his kisses trailed down my neck, and the fire it sparks feeling his hard dick pressed against me causes me to melt in his hands like an ice cream on a hundred and ten degree day in Texas. I crave him from my soul and the moment he releases me, I want it all over again. There is no such thing as enough when it comes to him.

"Girl I know you hear me talking to you!" Mya yells through the phone.

"I'm so sorry. I got carried away for a second."

"Ew, you know you're nasty, right?"

"Hell, I can't help it. Even after all these years, that man does something to me ,and I just can't get enough."

"So I've heard so many times before. Well, start with that." Her words trail off to a whisper.

"Wait, what was that last part?"

"Nothing. Just make the best of your weekend with him because you know we won't have a lot of time until after the holidays. This is going to be a really busy season this year. The holidays are coming up and people are doing Christmas and Black Friday shopping so there are gonna be hella loads to get out there."

"I know, and I'm not looking forward to it. If the summer was any indication, we are going to need all hands on deck. I may even pull Kacey in to help with a few drivers this time."

"Are you sure about that? You know the last time we did that she ended up making a shit show of all the loads and we lost a lot of money."

"Yeah, I've been letting her take a few trucks every now and then that is mine. You have those few that don't want to be handed off so I have to make sure they get their money. She knows if she messes up with them that's her ass, but she's gotten a lot better. I just can't put her in a panic mode and it will flow well."

Running this freight and dispatching company for the last three years has been a blessing and a curse. This was supposed to be mine and Markus' baby but it ended up being my baby. Finally getting all twenty of our trucks on the road and pushing loads for fifteen different trucking companies was something I couldn't do alone, so I had to hire some help. We have made good money with our company and Markus and I used to take a truck on the road on the weekends just to get away, but again that's something that died in the past. I have to leave that shit buried because he definitely won't be coming out of that office now to go over the road.

Having the real estate business has made him lazy. I helped him get all this shit started but it's like I don't exist to his ass anymore. He shut me out of the businesses he's running and left me to the ones I have, but I still miss my husband. I just want him back and running this freight business wouldn't be so bad.

"I know you have put a lot of faith in her. Just make sure you keep an eye on her."

"You know I will. I'm gonna go and get these tickets to this black and white party and try to find something good to have on the menu for the night. Hey, why don't you and Lance come to the black and white party? I know you don't want to wear a dress but come on it'll be fun."

"I'll think about it."

"Ok, I'll talk to you tomorrow at work."

The excitement boiling through my veins makes it hard for me not to pick up the phone to call Markus and tell him about the little plans I have for the weekend. I don't think this man knows how much I really love his red ass. I guess that's why I have to make the weekend one to show him what it is.

The sound of Markus walking up the stairs increases my heart rate and the flow of my blood through my veins fills my ears and my heart jumps into my throat. The nightstand lamp lighting up his face as he walks over to me makes me just that much more excited.

"Hey boo, how was your day?" he asks, planting double kisses on my lips. Damn, I miss his lips so soft, moist, and electric.

"It was alright. Can I ask you for something?"

"Anything babe. You know I got you."

"I want you to spend next Saturday with me. I have a few things planned to help us both relax and spend time together. What do you think?"

"Hell yeah you know I love spending time with you, baby," he said, pushing me back on the bed with his kisses. I can feel his length as it grows harder against my flower. Wet and all, I accept his invitation and allow him to open me up and pull my panties off.

His hand gripping my ass as he lifts me as though I'm a feather putting me in the middle of the bed. His dick is rock hard and doesn't need guidance to enter me, and my juices coat him as if his dick is dehydrated and begging for moisture. His teeth sink into my neck, sending a wave of pleasure through my pussy and instant ecstasy pulls the cum from my body, taking my soul with it. His light brown fiery eyes stare into mine and the slight smirk that blesses his face, and I know what just happened was all in his plan. Now it's time for the games to begin as he lowers himself between my thighs. His tongue dances on my clit and my body responds, filling his mouth with the sweet juices she produces for him, but he doesn't stop. I don't know how he does it but he makes his tongue vibrate against my clit and again my soul is his to do with as he pleases. Breathless, I hear his laugh accompany my heartbeat in my ears.

"Damn, baby, are you tapping out already?"

"No, no, no," I say, trying to gather myself while he's not taking me down.

"It looks like it," he says, his lips landing on mine.

"I'm not ready." I pant as his length starts to deposit inside me again.

"You're ready. You're always ready for me." His thrust was solid, smooth, and filling, taking my breath once again.

"Babe."

"Tell me this dick is good. Hm."

"Babe."

"Say it." His eyes never leave mine. "It's not good?" He goes deeper inside me.

"Your dick is good. It's good, baby."

I think I may have made to the wrong choice. The pace increases and trying to hold my cum is becoming hard to do. Every thrust is better than the last, and I see the determination and passion in his eyes. He loves making turns to straight fuckin', and I am loving every second of it.

"I can't, baby. I can't."

"You can't what? Hm."

"I can't hold it. I'm cumming, baby."

"I know it. I want you to cum dick," he says, sinking deeper with his length filling every part of me.

My mind fills with the days we met and the warm feeling his presence gave me, the look in his eyes as we stood before our families and officially became one, the love I felt spilling from him, the first time he made me feel like that was nothing or no one that could take my place. The desire and need comes through his touch. All of the emotions I have felt for this man consumes me ,and I release it all onto his dick.

"Damn, you know exactly what I need," I sputter out between breaths.

"I'm glad you got yours because that pussy is super wet, and I couldn't hold it no more." He lay next to me on the bed his body glistening with his sweat. "Now wipe me up babe so I can go to sleep."

"Man, nah, it's your turn."

"Alright, let's see who taps out first." He started to suck on my neck.

"Ok, ok, I'm going. I'm not ready for round two just yet."

Shaking the fuzzy haze from my mind to make sure I stay standing is harder than it's ever been. I don't know what's been on his mind at work, but he did his thang, read mine, and came through like the champ he is. I can never get rid of him. He is here to stay for sure.

****

Reeling from last night, I can barely keep my eyes open, but it's worth every second of the drowsiness and soreness I feel right now. The love that man gives is something I don't ever want to live without. I rub over the bed, trying to feel for the love of my life and he's not here. It never fails. It never lasts long, and I'm always left wondering why we can never wake up to one another. I pray this weekend time together will bring us closer together. I need my husband back. I need the man I love back in my life. These little drive-by fuck sessions ain't cutting it for me anymore.

With shades on and my hair pulled back in a bun, I make my way to the car to get this day started. I can honestly say though I feel the clouds under my feet carrying the weight I have been trying to lift from my shoulders. I still feel him inside me and his scent is still present in my nostrils, giving me life with every breath I take. Feeling the sun against my body reminds me of the warmth of his body heat on top of me. This man is something I can't shake.

Walking into my office I try to downplay the way I feel still with my shades on. "Good morning, no I don't want to talk but it would be great if someone can get me a cup of coffee." I let the door to my office close behind me.

I lay my head on the cold desk, but I can't shake this giddiness inside me. "Ok spill what's wrong with you?" Mya asks, bursting through the door.

"What?"

"Tell me. What the hell is going on with you?"

"Nothing. I'm just tired from last night. I went to bed late, and I should have taken my ass to bed."

"Yes, you should have taken your big booty ass to bed," a familiar male's voice said from behind Mya. The sound of his voice makes me wet all over again. "Who told you to leave the house without letting me know?"

"Hey baby, I thought you had already gone to work." I look up and see Markus standing at the door with food and flowers. "What are you doing here?"

"I'm bringing you the breakfast you were supposed to be served in bed. Now, Mya would you mind if I have a few minutes with my wife, please?"

While rolling her eyes so hard, I feel the annoyance coming from her she turns and with the perkiest voice I have ever heard her use saying, "Absolutely, you love birds have a good morning."

"Thank you, Mya," I say, winking at her as she turns to give me a stern face behind my husband's back.

"I miss you boo." Markus puts everything down on my desk before he walks around and kisses me.

"I miss you too. I love you."

"I love you more. So, you said last night you wanted us to spend next weekend together. What are we going to be doing?"

"It's going to be a surprise, but I promise we are going to have fun."

"Ok, I like that. I'm trusting you, and I know you know what I like."

"So can I have a replay of last night, tonight?"

"Nope, you can have better."

"I'm looking forward to it." I feel a slight tug on my bun and his lips covering mine with the passionate kiss he has given me. I crave this man in every way possible.

Watching him walk out the door, I look forward to tonight. I grab the box and pull a turkey sausage croissant from the box and take a big bite. I can see Mya making her way back to my office followed by Kacey, who's hot on her tail.

"Yes, ladies," I say with a small smile on my face.

"Now tell me what that was all about. He hasn't been here in forever. So what happened?"

"I got your coffee."

"Thank you, Kacey." I waited until she closed the office door behind her. "So last night, I didn't know what was going on but I liked it. I told Markus about the weekend and then he just made love to me and it was amazing."

"But you came in here like you were dying from a hangover or something."

"I was trying to hide it. I'm just on cloud one thousand." I laughed a little.

"Well, that's good. So have you finished planning out what you're going to do?"

"No, but I'm going to get it finished. I'm going to go get our formal wear tomorrow, and I think we are going to wear white or a mixture of the two somehow. Have you decided if you're going to go?"

"Yes, Lance said he wouldn't mind going so we are going to go too."

"Good, we can run into people together and it won't be awkward."

I try to spend the rest of the day focusing on getting these drivers their loads for the next two weeks. I have to make sure I have the money rolling in to pay for what I'm about to spend this weekend. I pray for this work and we will become close to the way we used to be.

****

The love of my life walks through the door, and I see the anger written all over his face. "Hey, babe how was your day?" I walk up to him wrapped in my robe with his favorite scent of mine on.

"Not good. I have to take care of some shit, and I don't know right now how I'm going to make this shit happen."

"Is there something I can do to help?" I ask, rubbing his back as I hugged him.

"No. I have to work this out on my own. I need access to the business account though."

"Why? For what?"

"I may need to pull from it."

"No, that's not going to work, considering we are going into our busy season, and waiting on invoices to be paid can put us in a bind that's why I have busted my ass to make sure I kept a certain amount untouched just in case."

"Look, Em, I don't have time for this right now. I need you to just do this for me. You said you want to help just give me the codes, and I'll put it back as soon as I have it available." With the panic and fear in his eyes, I know it's something bad going on, but I can't risk putting us in the red because he made some fucked-up choices.

"How much do you need?" I shouldn't have asked that. I know I shouldn't have. I know I'm not going to like the answer.

"I need five thousand dollars."

"For what?"

"Why? It doesn't matter. Are you going to give it to me or not?"

"I'll give it to you if you promise me you are going to make this weekend a priority."

"I can't promise you that. I have to handle this shit, and I don't know how long it's going to have me out."

"What do you mean have you out? Where the fuck are you going?"

"I'm not doing this right now. Are you giving me the fuckin' money or not?"

Feeling defeated and knowing that nothing I say from this point on is going to make a difference, I just gave up. "Yes, I'll send it to your account." I picked up my phone to transfer the money to him. I feel the tears sting my eyes and the hurt invade my bone, making them ache and the lump in my throat grow so big, I started to choke on it.

I make my way up the stairs before I let a single tear fall. I won't let him see what he has done to me. I won't let him have the satisfaction of knowing he has broken me. I won't let him know he has won. The fight in me for this is decreasing dramatically with every stupid argument and fight he can give two fucks about.

What happened to the man that wanted to know how he could fix his fucked-up ways? What happened to the man that hated to see me cry?

What happened to the man that promised to protect me from pain? I can't take this anymore.

I see him pacing the floor in the kitchen before I make my exit out the front door. I have to get away and clear my head. I don't look back as I get into the car and start the engine. I roll down all the windows and let the night air wash over me. I loosen my robe, taking in the air over my naked body. Tears make it difficult to see, but the level of not giving a fuck is so enormous right now that it could swallow the universe without hesitation. What did I do to make this man hate me so fuckin' much? Who did I fuck over in my past that made me become the victim of someone with this much hatred for me? What did I do to him? Why the fuck did I marry a man that doesn't or couldn't give two fucks about me, truly? I mean damn really is that easy for him to do this to me?

The sound of my phone ringing forced me to straighten up and put on a normal voice or as normal as I can muster. "Hello."

"Where are you?" Markus' voice rumbles calmly through the phone.

"Why? What do you care?"

"Stop playing with me, Em, and bring your ass home."

"I will later. I need time to think." I hang up the phone without giving him time to respond.

I can't believe this idiot has found me. I pull to the stoplight and see his car at the gas station facing the street. I can't escape for a damn minute without being hunted down. I keep looking ahead, but I can see the headlights start to come to my way and flicker at me from the corner of my eye. As soon as the light turns green, I am going to floor it because this is ridiculous. I drive through the stoplight, and I see him turning behind me, but there are a couple of cars between us. The phone rings again but answering is not an option right now. I keep going trying to turn corners to lose him, but no matter what he is right behind me. Without warning, he speeds around in front of me and slams on his brakes. I stop and watch as he walks back to the car.

"Where the fuck are you going?" Markus asked, anger dripping off of his every word.

"Can you get out of the way?"

"Open the door?"

"No, please move," I say and let the car roll forward.

Hitting the window he yells again, "Open the fuckin' door, Ember!"

I rolled down the window, "What do you want?"

"Take your ass home now," Markus said sternly, grabbing my face and never breaking eye contact.

Tears roll down my face and into his hand, causing him to let me go and his face to relax a bit. "I'm going."

I watch as he walks back to the car. I speed around him and make my way around the block trying not to let him see me and the way I end up going. This man has no shame in the way he makes me feel and the way he treats me. I pull into the driveway and rush inside the house. I strip out of the robe and start the shower. I hear the sound of the bedroom door closing, and I lock the bathroom door to prevent Markus from entering. I wash away the pain and the anger I have still roaring inside of me.

I step out into the bedroom, looking at Markus laying across the bed watching me move through the room. I climb into bed under the covers, and I turn my back to him. I can't help but let the tears flow. The pain is unbearable and the man I love lay next to me not giving a fuck about how I feel. The way he pretends to care about if I'm out with someone else makes it all the more painful. I mean damn I know you don't care, and I know it's only to make me feel a certain type of way. I know there is something else going on, I just don't know what it is, but it's making him turn me on to keep me what he calls in line..

I start to fall asleep when I feel Markus wrap his arms around me and pull me to him. I don't fight it. I just let him hold me and kiss me repeatedly on my cheek. I let myself drift off, lying to myself that he loves me and that one day he will come back to me.

*****

The water flowing from the running shower wakes me from the best dream I've had in a long time. I can't believe I feel like being with my husband is tearing me down like this. He is too comfortable with not giving a damn about me and my feelings, but he is still the love of my life.

Markus' phone buzzes against the nightstand, but I debate with myself about answering it. It wouldn't hurt for him to miss a few meetings since he wants to be an asshole to me. I grabbed the phone and facetime is ringing from an unsaved number. Answering it, I see the face of another woman who looks surprised to see her.

"Um…is Markus available?" the woman asks, looking uncomfortable.

"May I ask who you are?"

"I'll call back later." The woman ends the call before I have the chance to say anything to stop her.

I scroll through his messages and see messages going back for the last eight months and plenty of videos of him fuckin' her. The pain shot through me, and I couldn't stop the tears from falling. My heart is racing, my bones aching, my head pounding and my soul dies with every second I see the pictures of my husband with her children and with her as if he is not a married man. What is wrong with him and why is this so easy for him? I can't stay here, I can't continue in this relationship. Being lied to and mistreated is something I'm not going to tolerate. He can have this shit; no matter what the pain is to be had I accept it. Now I just have to plan a way to leave without all his bullshit.

Ember

I start my day carrying the weight of this bullshit in my head and my heart, but I have to make the best of it considering I have to meet with new clients today. I can't let this affect what I have to do. Since I will no longer be married, I have to make sure my finances are in order and I won't have to need him for anything once he is out of my life.

I leave the lights off in my office when I walk in, hoping to be left alone before it's time to go into my meeting. To take my mind off of the cheating, lying son of a bitch husband I go over the contracts again to make sure they are all in order. Half Moon Freight Inc. is one of the largest trucking companies in the state and securing this contract with them is going to take my company to another level. I can get this deal, but the fate of the universe seems to be working against me this morning. The messages start to come in back to back.

Markus: Why did you leave like that?

Markus: Did you go through my phone?

Markus: Em, I know you see my messages.

Markus: I have told you not to go through my shit and now you sitting over there with an attitude.

Me: Fuck you. You made your choice. You have a ready-made family so just pack your shit and leave me alone.

Markus: Don't fuck with me. If I leave I'm not going to leave that easy. You got me fucked up.

Me: Just leave me alone. You don't want me anyway, right?

Markus: Who is the nigga you fuckin' with? Whenever I find out who he is I'm going to kill both of y'all.

My office door swings open and an excited Mya follows it. "Mr. Dupree is here in the conference room." I guess the look on my face was something to cause her to worry. "What's wrong?"

"Nothing. I'm on my way." I close my laptop and take a deep breath, mentally preparing myself to close with this client.

The vibe in the room is bright enough to change the way I feel so I can let my nerves fall away since Mr. Dupree is all bright eyed and bushy tailed. I can honestly say seeing him in this light brings out a different level of attractiveness from him. Seeing him in jeans and a t-shirt with his little scruffy facial hair that hid the light in his eyes is nice, but the clean shaven, well dressed Dupree with his light brown eyes that brighten as he smiles is something I wasn't expecting.

"Good morning, Mr. Dupree. Thank you for meeting with me. I am looking forward to working with your trucking company," I say, shaking his well-manicured hand. Although his hands are bigger than mine, they feel warm and comforting.

"Good morning, and I'm glad to be here. You look amazing as always." I can see his eyes taking in my attire from head to toe.

"Thank you and you clean up nice as well."

"I appreciate it. I wanted to look nice for you," he said. The look in his eyes are seductive and flirty, making me blush.

"Well, Mr. Dupree, I am looking forward to this partnership, and we have some great incentives. Along with heaving the factoring company that will help secure payment faster than waiting for the brokers to pay out, we have gas cards for every truck that you have assigned to us. We have trip planning for the duration of the driver's desired time to be on the road. Each load will be top paying loads, and we will honor the request for the dollars per mile, but the only exception will be if the distance is close and to prevent deadheading," I start to explain after clearing my throat, trying to get us back on track.

"Mrs. Ballard, I'm not worried about anything, and I know I'm in good hands. I came here ready to sign the contract and ready to work with you long term. You had me on board from day one, I just needed to properly end the previous contract." His smile drips hard with the flirting.

"Well that's good to know, and how many trucks are we going to be covering? I want to also remind you the contract is for three years. After, we can resign for the same or just continue to work with one another on a month-to-month basis but working month-to-month will cause an increase in the percentage we take for each load," I reiterate the terms of the contract.

"That's completely fine. We have ten trucks eight of which are CDL and two non-CDL. Where do I sign?"

As I point to the highlighted places for him to sign and hand him the onboarding packet, I look up to see a very angry Markus walking through the office, frantically looking for me. I glanced at Mya and back at Markus in the lobby, trying to signal her to handle him while I finish with Mr. Dupree. She finally catches my line of vision and exits the room.

"Ok, so when can we get started?"

"We are actually going to get started today. I need all the contact information for all of the drivers, the license plate number to assign the truck a number, and to know where they all are so we can pick up where they are and get them to their next destination."

"Em, we need to talk." Markus burst through the conference room door with Mya looking defeated at trying to stop him.

"Markus, I'm in a meeting." That was a mistake because his attention went from me to Mr. Dupree.

"Hi, I'm Gavin Dupree." He holds his hand out for Markus to shake.

"Markus Ballard." Still shooting daggers at Mr. Dupree, he reluctantly shakes his hand.

"Oh, so you are the lucky man that has this beauty on his arm. You are a lucky man," Mr. Dupree says, not fazed by the look Markus is giving him.

"That right. I'm her husband. Now Em, we need to talk."

"Go ahead, Mrs. Ballard, I'll be here when you are finished." Mr. Dupree takes his seat again.

"I apologize, and I will be back as soon as I can." I grab Markus by the hand and lead him out of the conference room and to my office, not saying a word until the door closes behind him. "Are you trying to tank this deal for me? I am trying to keep my business going." I raise my voice.

"What do you mean your business? So is this not something that we share anymore?"

"No, Markus, we don't share this anymore. You made your choice when you decided you wanted to cheat. So, go be with your woman and leave me alone." I step around him and return to my meeting.

"Who is this man? It looks like it's more than business between the two of you. Don't make me knock his ass out!"

"Markus, how can you be mad because another man is seeing what you have obviously forgotten? This is a business meeting and something important to me. Now if you don't mind, I would like to get back to it."

"I'm going to wait right here until you're finished and don't take all day because I have shit to do."

"Whatever." I walk out of the office and quickly make my way back to the conference room where Mya is keeping Mr. Dupree on ice. "Ok, where were we?"

"I have gotten everything you have requested and once you are done here, we can get the driver distributed. Mr. Dupree here requested to be added to your list of drivers. I didn't know what your load looked like at the moment, so I didn't confirm or deny anything."

"Thank you, Mya, and Mr. Dupree I would be happy to add you to the roster. The cards for the drivers will be ready in about ten days from Friday, and we will have them mailed to your office."

"Thank you, Mrs. Ballard. I can't wait to see what this journey with you and your company will hold."

"Likewise, and welcome to the Royal family." I shake his hand, picking up the paperwork from the table.

After seeing Mr. Dupree out of the building, I brace myself for the bullshit Markus is about to try and throw at me with his selfish ass. What the entire fuck does he expect to happen when he cheats? I'm not standing for it, and he's gonna have to suck this shit up and take it to his new woman's house. I stare at him until I walk in and the look on his face just makes me want to slap the shit out of him.

"Now what do you want, Markus? I have a lot of work to do and sitting here talking to you about something I have made up my mind on won't get the shit done," I say, walking around my desk to my chair. "And get your ass out of my chair."

"Who do you think you're talking to, Em? Why did you go through my phone?"

"What difference does that make? You are still fuckin' up and cheating." I raise my voice.

"If you would have stayed in your place and not violated my privacy, then you wouldn't have known shit about what's going on in my phone."

"So you're telling me it's my fault that you are cheating ass nigga with community dick. Is that what you're telling me right now? I think you have to be the most delusional muthafucka on this planet."

"Watch your fuckin' mouth," he says, his eyes turning a light shade of red from rage, but the ringing of his phone turns his attention from me.

"You better go see what your wife wants before she gets mad because you are ignoring her calls." I make sure to cover every word in sarcasm.

"You better watch your mouth, and we're not done with this shit," he says, walking to the door and almost knocking Mya over as he rushes past her.

As a wide smile spread across her face, Mya takes a seat across from me. "So, I know this may not be on your mind right now, but I was thinking about what you said about the weekend trip."

"What weekend trip?" The tape recorder in my head instantly starts to replay conversations we have had in the past.

"You know you said if you got the contracts then we would all take the weekend off and go on a trip. So, where are we going?"

"Well, I think you are being a little hasty because we have only gotten one contract signed. We still need Edward Roundtree to sign the contract to join and pray he is bringing in at least seven trucks to get us to the quota."

"You know you are going to have him eating out of the palm of your hand like Dupree was, and what's with this quota of yours?"

"If we can maintain eighty-five trucks along with our fifteen trucks, then we will have one hundred trucks running year round for the next three years. Yes, we are going to have some slow months, but that's why we are going to work hard to make sure we stay on top of these loads. Sometimes, they may not go where they want to go, but hey they will be bringing home a paycheck every week. Which to me is all that matters."

"Ok, so where are we going?"

The ping from my phone takes my attention as I read the message that displays on the screen.

Markus: I'm not playing with you, Em. You're not leaving me.

I don't know why he is playing like he just really wants me around when he has made the choice to be with this other woman. I mean so much so that he didn't even try to hide the shit. Fuck him. I don't deserve this shit. I am too good to his ass for him to treat me like this and still turn the tables on me like it's my fault that he decided to go stick his dick in another bitch.

"Girl. I know you hear me talking to you."

"My bad, but where do you want to go? I think I want to go somewhere that's warm but not just scorching hot all day."

"That sounds good, but what about Vegas? I have never been and you know what they say. What happens in Vegas stays in Vegas, and I think it would be good for you to cut loose a little bit."

"You know what, you might be right. Now we just need to decide on the weekend we will go," I say, still thinking about the fucked-up shit that's making my life fall apart.

*****

Walking into the house, the vibe even feels fucked. Relaxing is the last thing I'm gonna be able to do until I remove the tension from here. Hell, at least I don't have to wonder where the fuck he is anymore. I know he's stuck under this bitch or has his dick embedded inside of her. I still can't believe I'm surprised that this is the type of nigga he turned out to be. I just have to stick to my guns and end this marriage and take care of myself. No more looking out for other people and putting me last.

I make my way through the empty house and enter my bedroom, shedding my clothes from the door all the way to the bathroom. Naked, I start the shower and I pray this hot water washes the bullshit of me. I lather my washcloth and rub it across my body, washing the pain, anger, heartbreak, and envy off and down the drain. I let the tears fall involuntarily and let the water mask them. I have to get it all out now so nothing he says will make me change my mind. I can't let him keep having this hold on me; I have to take back this control he finds so valuable to have and letting him see he has hurt me will only confirm he still has it. I can't let that happen.

Still dripping wet, I walk into the closet and slip into my silk green robe and my olive green fur slippers, feeling better than I have all day. I take the stairs down to the kitchen to grab my bowl of fruit from the fridge and a little sugar to cover it in. It's cold and sweet and will feed this beast of depression that's attempting to roar out of me.

My bed calls me like a magnet pulling something metal to it. I return to my room and start watching *Deadly Women*. Now they have the right idea. Hell, their only downfall was getting caught, but sometimes that's what these men need. A damn good killing. I hear his sigh come through the door before he does but acknowledging him is not what he will get tonight.

"Babe, do you know the truck is paid off? I think we should go ahead and get the Audi you've been waiting for," Markus says, walking over to the bed. He leans down and tries to kiss me, but I lay over on the pillow that's next to me, never taking my eyes off the TV. "So you still have an attitude? Come on, baby, don't do me like this. I love you, and I'll get my shit together."

I look at him out of the corner of my eye because I know all that shit is a lie. "Really? You're going to get your shit together? What are you going to do or not do?" I ask, looking back at the TV while waiting for another lie to fall from his face.

"I don't have to get into it, but you know what it is. We are going to make this work. Alright."

"That's sad that you can't even say the fucked-up shit that you are doing. I mean is it that hard for you to say I'm cheating on you and I'm going to stop? Or are you just telling me that so I can get off your back while you keep doing the bullshit? Which is it?" I ask, feeling the thump of my heart in my chest increase and become harder.

I force the tears to dry as I blink them away and swallow the lump in my throat that forces dread through my veins. The pain is starting to be unbearable and I can't. I just can't. I return my attention to the TV. I wish so badly I could get away with taking his ass down for hurting me like this. I don't want to love him anymore.

"I didn't say that I couldn't, but what's the point of saying it when you know what it is that we're talking about?"

"I don't want to talk about it." I get up, stalk to the closet, and slam the drawers as I ravage through them looking for something to wear. I pull on my jeans and a sweater.

"If you want me to say what I'm doing wrong, you need to say what you have done wrong in the past."

"What the fuck are you talking about?" I ask, shoving my foot into my shoe so hard I feel the pain shoot through my foot up to my ankle.

"You know you have been messing around on me in the past. You have had niggas you have talked to and been with, and I know you done fucked."

"Markus get the fuck out of here with that stupid shit. You are so caught up in trying to cover up your bullshit that you can't help to try and find a way to make this shit my fault. I haven't done anything but been mistakenly loyal to an disloyal husband. And to think that's what you claim to be about."

"You don't have to lie to me. I know what you have done. I have people everywhere, and they told me what you have done and what kind of woman you are. I looked past that and still love you, but you keep bringing up this shit and I told you that it's over."

"I'm not about to do this with you." I grab my keys from the bedside table and ran downstairs and out the door to my car. I can't let him see me this way and then he will think he has won.

"Em. You can't keep running away from this shit. Come back in this house now."

I close the door, lock, and start the car. He stands in front of the car, looking at me. "Move your ass out of the way!" I yell, trying to hold the tears back from falling.

"Come in the house, babe. I'm through." He walks to the driver's side door.

"No." I pull the car into drive and drive out onto the street.

The lights in the city whip past me as my vision blurs and clears with the tears filling my eyes and falling away. I let the pain consume me and ache to the depths of my heart and snatch my soul into the darkest corner inside. I'm tired of being hurt, and by a nigga that couldn't give two fucks about the damage he's causing. I can't stand the fact that this is the man that I have given my everything to. I have poured so much of myself into him to make him feel accomplished and this is the thanks I get from him.

I pull into the parking lot of Betty Ann's Soul Food Kitchen and look into the window of the business, debating about going inside. I need to take some time to let my feelings settle and sort out my thoughts, but I want to be left alone. The parking lot is almost empty so I guess the dinner rush is over. I look around once more before stepping out and making my way to the door.

I'm greeted by the hostess at the podium once inside. "Good evening, how many?"

"Just one. Thank you."

"Would like a booth or a table?"

"Can I have the booth at the very back in the corner, please?" I ask, looking at the dimly lit corner.

"Yes, follow me this way please."

I glance around at the people sitting around eating and talking with each other. Watching the couples having a great time makes me feel a ping of envy and heartache. I was supposed to be loved like that. I was supposed to be happy with the man I vowed to spend the rest of my life with, but here I am trying to figure out how to shake this marriage and never have to look at this man in his face again.

I send Mya a quick text.

Me: Hey do you mind coming to have a drink with me? My treat.

Mya: But you don't drink.

Me: I think I'm about to start.

Mya: I'm on my way. Where are you?

Me: Betty's

Maybe getting drunk for the first time in my life is just what I need to take my mind off of the bull crap flooding my life right now. Maybe I can pretend my husband loves me.

*****

I wake up again to an empty bed and surprisingly, I don't feel anything. I think the last few days of ignoring him have done me some good. I'm numb to his absence among other things he does daily to hurt me. I have to find a divorce lawyer before he tries to wiggle his way back in good with me.

Google is full of divorce lawyers, but Kraig Morton seems to have the best reviews so Mr. Morton it is. I dial the number with my heart racing and my hand trembling. I am nervous, and I don't know what to expect.

"Good morning, thank you for calling the Law Office of Morton and Crim. How can I help you?"

"Good morning, my name is Ember Ballard, and I need to set a time for consultation to start my divorce."

"OK, who do you prefer Kraig Morton or Allen Crim?" the receptionist asks.

"Mr. Morton, please."

"Ok, the earliest appointment he has open is Friday at ten."

"That's perfect, thank you."

Markus walks into the kitchen where I have made myself comfortable researching lawyers and drinking my coffee. I close my laptop as he walks over to me at the kitchen table.

"Good morning," Markus speaks, leaning over to kiss me. Nope, not today Satan. I grab my laptop and walk out of the kitchen.

"Ok, Mrs. Ballard, I have you down for Friday at ten. Have a great rest of your day." I walk up the stairs with him walking two steps behind me.

"So, you're still on your bullshit. What is it going to take for you to get past this? I can't keep living like this. You have been walking around here like I don't exist for days."

"Well I'm sorry, but I don't have anything to say to you." I lay the computer on the bed and walk into the closet.

I hear him tapping away on my laptop, but I've changed the password to get in.

"Open the laptop Em," he demands from the bedroom.

"For what?" I pull on a pretty green jumpsuit and white and green air max.

"I need to use it for a second."

"No, you have your shit so use it." I walk out of the closet and grab my computer from him and my keys from the nightstand to leave.

"Em, what the fuck is wrong with you?"

I stopped in the doorway, fighting back tears. "I don't feel safe with you anymore. You used to be the one I thought would push me to keep moving forward, the one to love me and be different from everything I have been through. Unfortunately, though you turned out to be worse than the son of a bitch that used to beat my ass."

"How is that?"

I turn to face him and can see him swallow hard. "Because you know everything that I have gone through. I opened myself up to you and told you things that I hadn't even dealt with myself. I told you about my emotional and physical abuse. I told you why I don't have a family, but guess what you do? You use it all against me. You make me out to be the bad guy and blame me for the many fucked-up ways you have. You have put your hands on me and most importantly, I have to compete for you when you were supposed to be mine, and I lose every time. I'm tired of this, and I know deserve better and I will have better. You don't have to support my dreams and goals because I will. You don't have to encourage me to do anything because I will encourage myself. You don't have to love me because I love me." I say the last part almost in a whisper. I can't hold this back anymore. I let him see the pain he has caused since telling him doesn't seem to be enough.

"Em, I'm sorry, and I will get it together. I promise. I am so sorry." He briskly walks toward me and wraps me in his arms. I hear his uneven breathing and his body trembles.

I sob so hard into him for a minute. I hold him so tight silently praying he is going to change. I pray he is going to be the man that he said he was going to be to love me and treat me right.

We lay in bed together when his phone rings. He looks at the display, takes a deep sigh, and gets up. I turn my attention back to the TV as he walks into the bathroom to take the call. I don't know where this is going to go, but I hope he does the right thing.

I let myself fall asleep to the sound of the water from the shower, and I let it overcome me and take me. *I walk into the room and see Markus sitting on the sofa talking on the phone, acting none the wiser that I'm there in the same room. The music softly plays in the background slow and romantic.*

"Yes, baby I will be home soon. I just have to tie up some loose ends, and I'll be there as soon as I can."

"Markus!" I try to get his attention to avail, but he can't hear me.

"Baby, I know you are hungry and I am going to feed the baby. Just give me a few minutes, and I will take you wherever you want."

There I am walking into the room with two glasses of wine with the biggest smile on my face. This man can't do any wrong in my eyes, and I just know he is doing everything he is supposed to do.

I hand him his glass and lay my leg across his lap as I sit down on the sofa next to him. "Who is that on the phone?" I ask.

"I have to go." He ends the call abruptly. "Nobody, just some work stuff. You know how it gets this time of year. I have to make sure everybody is staying on top of their shit."

"Well you know if you need me I got you," I say, looking at him lovingly. "You know I told you I have a surprise for you, right? Well, I have to show you something." I pull the pregnancy test from my pocket and hand it to him.

"What is this?"

"Look at it. What does it look like?"

"Is this for real?" The look on his face spells it all out for me to see and there is no mistake about how he feels, but it seems like I am in denial because the smile never leaves my face. "I don't know what to say."

"Aren't you happy? This is what we always wanted, right? We have been trying for a baby and now are about to have one," I excitedly say to him.

"Yes, this is what we have always wanted," he says with a half-smile. His phone rings in his hand. "I have to go, babe. This is work. I know this is supposed to be our night together, but they need me."

The pain of defeat is written all over my face, but as always I put on a smile and accept his word for what it is. I watch as he rushes out of the door without a second look behind him. The light from the outside *shine blindingly to change the room. I blink to adjust my eyes to the lights and notice I'm standing in Markus' office, looking at him holding his head in his hands crying. His friend, Aaron, sat across from him looking extremely sympathetic.*

"Have you talked to her? I mean since she has left?" Aaron asked, leaning forward.

"No, and I can't get anyone to get her to talk to me. I mean I just need to talk to her. I can't believe I let her go and thought I would find someone like or better than her. I was stupid as fuck," Markus says almost in a full blown sob.

"You are only upset because she got tired of waiting for you to change and love her the way she loved you. You wanted your cake and eat it too when you saw the one you chose wouldn't do half the shit your wife did, you couldn't process it. You should have known there was nothing there in that relationship because her drive was nothing compared to what your wife had. She supported you in everything when you let her dreams fall by the wayside as if they meant nothing. That woman deserves the world and you couldn't even give her the crust between your toes," An unknown man says, standing at the door, watching the two of them looking crazy. "Aaron, what's going on with you?"

"I can only imagine how he feels, and I have seen how she was with him. It bothers me to know they won't be together because they were an awesome couple, and I know they could have set this city on fire."

"He set it on fire alright, and it burned his whole life to the ground." The man chuckles. "You better hope I can't find her and make her mine because you will see what can happen when you love a woman right."

Markus looks up and starts to scream and run toward the man with the glare of death in his eyes.

I sit straight up in the bed, panting, sweating, still shaking with fear. I look over and the bed is empty but the bathroom light is on, and I walk to the door to hear what's going on.

"You know I had to tell her something to get her to calm down. If I hadn't, then what? I have the other house, but I have too much invested over here and I need to see it through," Markus says. The faint voice of a woman speaks to him, and just the sound of her voice hurts my feelings.

I thought he was going to change. I thought he was going to leave her alone and fix us, our relationship, our trust, but I guess again I gave him too much credit. I listen again as he starts to speak.

"Look, you are who I want to be with and I'm looking into having her served with divorce papers as soon as this quarter is over and I know everything is going as planned."

I wipe the tears from my eyes and climb back into bed, covering my head with the covers and letting the pain consume me. This has got to be what it feels like to die because there is no way to come back from this.

*****

I sit behind my office desk with my mirror out, trying to put makeup on my puffy eyes and drink coffee to wake up from the sleepless night I've had. The meeting with Mr. Roundtree will take place in an hour, and I have to get myself together.

Mya walks in and places a file on my desk. "Are you ready?"

"As ready as I'm going to be," I reply to her.

"Wait a minute what's going on with you?" She looks at me. "Have you been crying?"

"Markus is cheating on me and he lies to me constantly. He makes me beg to be with him and he without regard for how I feel puts his mistress before me. I have heard him talking to her in the bathroom about seeing something through. I don't know what he's talking about, but he is very adamant about it." I let it all out, not sparing her from the sobs I let out throughout the whole thing.

"Hey, hey, hey we are going to get through this." Mya hands me a tissue and rubs my back standing next to me.

"I know. I am going to see a divorce attorney, and I'm going to take all of the businesses since they all belong to me. He has nothing with his name on it, and I intend to take what's mine. He doesn't care about me and how I feel so I will take it ,and he can apply for a job to work for me," I say, giving a little laugh.

"Well, that's one way to make him feel the burn," Mya says. "Whatever you need help with I'm here for you."

My phone vibrates on the corner of my desk. "I can't believe he is calling me right now."

"Don't answer."

"If I don't answer, he is just going to keep calling until I do." The phone stops ringing and almost instantly starts to ring again. "See." I roll my eyes and answer. "What?"

"We need to talk," Markus says.

"No, we don't. Goodbye."

"Don't hang up this damn phone. Get to the house, Em, so we can talk."

"No, I have work to do."

"See I know you are probably sitting there with Mya's messy ass listening to her. She probably got another nigga waiting on you, don't she?"

"Markus will you stop with your bullshit. I don't have time. I have a client coming in so I have to go."

Before he can say anything, I hang up and put on my best smile for the tall handsome green-eyed man walking toward my office with a beaming smile on his face ready to talk business.

Markus

I can't believe she is putting me through all this shit. Hell, it's not like I'm asking the other bitch to marry me. I can't help she has fallen in love with me. The front door opens and closes, and I know Ember is running away from this again. I can't let her leave. Every time she goes out the door, it kills me a little inside not knowing if she's going to come back.

"Em, baby wait!" I yell, running down the driveway to her car. By the smell of rubber burning and the sound of her tires screeching I know she is doing her damnest to get away from me as fast as she can.

I didn't mean to hurt her and hell, if she would do some of the things I like then we wouldn't be going through this. I just need someone I can relate to, and she doesn't do anything. I just want my wife to want to go out and have fun.

I watch after her as my phone starts to vibrate in my pocket. My mind is telling me to let her be but my heart is telling me to go after her. The phone starts to vibrate again, and I look to see Aaron's name on the screen.

"Hey, man what's up?" I ask, looking back in the direction Em had gone before heading back to the house.

"I don't mean to bother you, man, but I need your help with something. Do you think you can come over?" Aaron asks.

"Yeah, I'll be there in fifteen." I rush him off the phone. I scroll through my contacts to bae and tap it, calling Ember.

"You've reached Ember Ballard. Please leave-" her voicemail picks up.

The sound of her voice still makes my heart flutter. Why can't I just have her and it is enough? I know she loves me, and I know she's not doing anything, but there is something inside me that's telling me other men want my wife. Other men talk to her and flirt with her, and I don't know if she has the willpower to turn down every man she sees. I mean there is going to be one man that is better than me and he is going to take her. I can't let the thought of losing her break me.

Aaron is sitting on his porch with a cooler and a beer in his hand. His face lights up as I get out of the car. He scoops his hand into the cooler, pulls out a cold one and sticks it out to me.

"I thought you could use a breather. How is the wife?" Aaron asks, relaxing into his chair again.

"The wife is still pissed off about Lynn. I don't know how, but she knows I haven't cut her off, and Em doesn't hide how she feels about it."

"Have you considered cutting Lynn off? I mean, to be honest, what can she do for you?"

"I don't need her to do anything for me."

"Right, because Ember is doing everything for you. What value does Lynn bring to your life? The better question is what has Ember done to make you feel that she isn't worth your respect and love?" Aaron asks, looking serious. I can't lie, he has a point, but I can't help myself. I don't want to let go of this. This is my escape from the arguing and fighting that Em and I have.

"I know what you mean, but I just can't stop, man." My phone vibrates on my cooler with Lynn's number displayed across the screen. "Hello."

"Hey, baby, are you coming home tonight?"

"Yeah, I'll be over. Why? What's up?" I ask.

"I'm cooking, and I just wanted to make enough for you if you were coming by."

"Yeah, I'll be there soon."

"Ok, I love you," Lynn says before ending the call.

"See, that's what I mean," Aaron says after I lay the phone back down on the cooler.

"What?"

"You don't even have her name saved to her number in your phone. I don't want to hear that shit about you don't want Em to know which number is hers because I can most definitely guarantee Em has her number since the first time you let it slip that you have been fuckin' her. Do you think this is the first time she has noticed that number? She just hasn't said anything until now."

"That shit doesn't matter, and Em couldn't have known about her. Em is very emotional, and she lets it out when she is angry and especially when she's upset. She doesn't hold that shit back."

"You have a lot to learn. You are about to lose a good woman and what you get in return is going to make you wish you had done her right. Take it from me, I've been there and done that."

"I have to go. This girl is about to cook, and I'm gonna go at least see what she is cooking."

"Why? Em cooks for you every night even when she's mad at you. So, I guess that means you're going to eat twice to make sure you don't cause any more issues with Em?" Aaron asks, shaking his head. "This shit is going to catch up with you. Everything you are doing has a price and you are gonna have to pay it," he says, throwing his head back and finishing his beer.

The sound of Em's voice plays in my head. *"You are going to reap what you sow. I have been good to you, and God is going to whip your ass for hurting me. I am a blessing for you as you were supposed to be for me, but you have shattered that."*

I can't lose my wife, but this is more complicated than anyone knows. How can I choose between two people I love?

On the car ride over to see Lynn, I can't help but list out their qualities in my head. On paper, Lynn has Em beat, but that's on paper.

Em, on the other hand, has constantly shown me her worth and how she can build me up. It's not all talk with her. She has pulled me out of some shit, but there is always something going wrong and delaying what we have planned. That shit gets old fast, and I won't keep putting my faith in that shit.

I pull onto Lynn's street and see the kids playing in the street. I honk and they come running to the car. Lynn has two kids, a boy and a girl; they are bad as hell but they are young enough to where I know they won't do shit to hurt me.

"Hey Markus, can you take us to the store?" the boy asks. He is a chubby something and always wants something. He's a cool kid though.

"Yeah, I'll take y'all to the store real quick."

"Markus, can I get some marshmallows?" the little girl asks, climbing into the backseat of the car.

"If they have them at the convenient store."

The store run takes us all of ten minutes since lil' momma couldn't make up her mind about which gummies she wanted to get. Pulling back into the driveway, Lynn is fuming while looking for them, but she visibly relaxes when she sees them get out of the car with me.

"What the hell did I tell y'all? The next time y'all run off without telling me I'm gonna beat ya ass!" she yells as they run into the house with their bag of snacks. "Hey, you. You could have told me they were with you," she said, kissing me on the lips.

"They were already playing on the street. I didn't think it would make much of a difference."

"Well I got you a bottle, and I have cooked fried chicken and mac and cheese. So come on so you can eat."

I don't know where the night has gone, but I know my head is killing me, and I can't open my eyes because of the sun beaming through the window. Shit, shit, shit…I grab my phone and see thirty missed calls and a bunch of messages from Em. Damn, I fucked up. I fucked up.

I grab my clothes and throw them on, trying to shake the drumming in my head. I leave without saying anything. Hell, if my marriage wasn't over before it's for sure over now. This is the deal breaker for Em. She has always said never let the sun beat me home and that muthafucka is up and dancing a happy dance across the morning sky. Fuck, I can't believe I've done this shit.

The fear runs cold through my body as I look at the front door that stands before me. I don't have a legitimate excuse for not coming home last night, and she is going to be able to smell my lies from a mile away. I take a deep breath and steady myself before walking into the house.

I walk into the house and it's eerily quiet. "Em, baby." I walk through the living room and into the kitchen, and she's nowhere to be found. I hear the TV upstairs playing and I head that way, bracing myself for the wrath that's about to come down on my head.

I step into the dark room. The curtains are drawn tight, the TV is playing, and Em lays bundled under the covers. "Em, baby." I pull the cover from around her to try and wake her up. The hospital bracelet appears around her wrist, and I'm instantly overcome with regret. Something happened to my wife, and I wasn't there when she needed me.

"Damn, what have I done?" I whisper, trying not to wake her. I can't face her right now. I just can't.

I quietly make my way into the shower, letting the water wash over my head, trying to take away the guilt I have inside me. I can only imagine what was going through her head while she was sitting in the hospital trying to get ahold of me. I love her so much, and yet I can't stop hurting her. Every day I walk into the room I see the pain in her eyes, the desire to receive the love she deserves, but here I am being the selfish asshole, making her feel like shit because I know she loves me too much to leave.

I have to be here for her. She needs me so much right now and pulling away from her isn't the right thing to do. I let the water drip off until I make it to the bedroom. I watch her laying there her cocoa brown skin, looking soft as silk with her brownish black hair pulled up into a bun, letting the sweet round of her face expose her beauty. She is the most amazing woman in the world, and I know it deep down in my soul and yet this is the bullshit I'm doing to her.

I towel off and climb into bed with her. "I'm so sorry, baby. I should have been there for you. I'm sorry," I let a tear fall while whispering to her. I can't keep hurting her. I just hope it's not too late for us.

The smell of food fills my nostrils, waking me to find my baby is not lying next to me. I take my ass downstairs to see her moving around the kitchen the way she does when she's excited about something. My baby loves to cook and be in the kitchen and it makes me happy to see her being herself again.

"Something smells good," I say, walking behind her and wrapping my arm around her waist.

Pulling out of my grip, she says, "Thank you. I just wanted a nice breakfast today."

"Em, I'm sorry about last night. I fell asleep in Aaron's driveway after we had been drinking. I lost track...."

"It's fine. I understand," she says with a small smile on her face as she starts to plate our breakfast.

"Em, I don't like us being like this. I want us back, and I want you to be happy to see me again."

"I am happy to see you."

"But you don't love me the same. I can feel it."

"Yeah, but that's because in a relationship you grow and a lot of things change. So the love for you has changed to fit the current status of our relationship," she explains as my face twists in confusion.

"And what is the status of our relationship right now?"

"I'm not sure yet. I mean if you know you can tell me," she says, placing both plates on the kitchen table before sitting down.

I watch her as she eats her breakfast, wondering what switch has been flipped to make her change her attitude. Something is off; I can feel it, and I don't think it's going to end well for one or both of us if I don't fix this shit.

After breakfast, I couldn't just be sitting in the house and wonder what she is planning or what she has said fuck it to in order not to have any emotions about what's going on anymore.

Julian walks into my office. "Hey, man I have the reports you have been looking for. I think you are going to be happy when you look at the numbers."

"Thank you," I say, leaning back in my chair.

"What's going on with you, man?"

"To be honest, I don't know. You know I have been fuckin' with the little bitch, Lynn, for a minute now. Well, Em found out and at first, she went ape shit crazy on me, but now she's acting like everything is all good. I fucked up last night and stayed out all night, and she ended up in the hospital. I tried to explain, but she just blew me off."

"What did she go to the hospital for?"

"I don't know. I was so messed up about her new attitude that I didn't even get the chance to ask while we were eating breakfast."

"Wait, she cooked breakfast? And you ate it?"

"Yeah, that's one thing she's not gonna do. She loves to make food and that is one of her love languages so she wouldn't kill me doing something she loves to do."

"You'll be surprised sometimes."

"I just don't know how to stop fuckin' off on her, and I know she is the best thing that has ever happen to me, but still I give her all this shit to deal with daily."

"You have to be the dumbest man I have ever met. You telling me this woman is the best thing that has ever happened to you but you can't love and respect her enough to be faithful? I don't understand that logic. I guess you'll figure it out once she leaves you."

"She's not going to leave me. She loves me."

"Every woman has her breaking point and you have been fuckin' off since day one. You will see one day when another man has her on his arm doing the things you wanted to do with her."

I feel the rage boiling in my chest, but I can't be mad at him because it's all true. There isn't a lie in anything he said, but again I can't find it in my heart to stop. I grab my phone and walk out of my office.

"Where are you going, Markus?"

"I have to go home and be with my wife before I not have one."

I flow through traffic, trying my best to avoid getting on the freeway and getting stuck in a traffic jam. I have to make it home to see what's going on with my wife. There is something seriously wrong, and I need to know what it is. I can't believe I'm losing control like this.

I don't waste any time running upstairs to find her. I don't know what has her so defeated and tapped out, but she needs me. I undress and climb into the bed with her.

"Baby, can we talk?" I ask, sliding close to her.

"Yes, we can talk. What do you want to talk about?" she asks, never taking her eyes from the TV.

"I want to know what I can do to make this right. Tell me what happened to make you go to the hospital."

"I passed out in the store and because I have you as my 'in case of an emergency' contact they called you. Once I was in the hospital they told me you wouldn't answer Mya tried to call and message you and you still didn't answer. It is what it is. I'm not fucked-up about it anymore."

"I'm sorry. I was drunk, and I fell asleep in the car."

"Look, I don't need an explanation. You made your choice and I wasn't it so fuck it."

"So, we got the project at work and we have it all sorted out since we have the numbers from last quarter. We made enough to push through and still stay afloat."

"That's good. I'm glad you are making progress," she said, sounding as if she doesn't give a damn about our business at all.

I wrapped my arms around her and pulled her close. I feel her body tense up, but I don't care. I want to hold my wife and hold her I shall. She lets out a deep sigh, but she doesn't move.

"I love you, Em."

Three

Lynn

This shit is for the birds, and I don't know how I am going to get rid of this bitch so I can have my man for myself. I don't want to keep waiting until he is supposed to get whatever he is supposed to be getting from her to leave. I want my man to be home with his new family and leave the bullshit behind.

"I don't think I can do it anymore, Tangy. I mean I think I have been patient enough dealing with this shit for the last eight months and then on top of that, I had to get an abortion the first time he got me pregnant because he didn't want there to be anything to hang over his head when he filed for his divorce. Am I wrong?"

Tangy has been my friend for the last year or so since we have been working together at the warehouse in town. She has a kind of con artist attitude, but she hasn't done anything for me not to like her.

She looks at me kind of surprised. "Girl you know he is going to do what makes his wife happy. I mean they are still married and what she wants is what's going to happen. I don't think you should get your hopes up about him leaving her until he shows you the paper and she has been served with them."

"I hear what you are saying, but he said that he is only there to get what he started finished, and then he was going to set things into motion. Now I don't have any reason not to believe him because he's always here and when she calls, he doesn't answer the phone. He pays her no attention when he is here. He even spends the night only to get up in the morning to go work."

Tangy kind of rolls her eyes. "He is going to tell you whatever it takes to keep you on ice so you won't leave, and he is probably doing the same to her. If you want him to be with you then you need to just not give him a choice. Have you even told him you're pregnant?"

"Yes, he knows I'm pregnant."

"What I want to know is what is it that he is waiting on the happen that he can't leave? What is it that he does again?"

"They have a business that his wife is running, and he doesn't want to go through with a divorce until he at least has his name on the business so she can't take all of the profits or something. I think he wants her to be the one to pay alimony when they get a divorce. Hell, he has already convinced her to put his name on all the cars so when he leaves, he will take them and I will get the new truck she just bought."

"Damn, y'all are some coldhearted muthafuckers. I think you better watch out for him. I mean if he will do this to his wife the one he took vows with and said he would love forever, he won't hesitate to do you the same way if not worse," Tangy says, giving me a concerned look.

"You know nothing. That man loves me and he even takes her money to pay my bills and feed my kids. He doesn't want or love her. He is just tying up some loose ends," I explain, getting more upset with each word spoken by her about the man she loves.

"Look, I understand you love him, but I just want you to be careful and happy," Tangy says.

"Ok fuck all that, I need you to take me to Markus' office. I was supposed to have lunch with him."

"Are you sure? I don't want to take you there and he's too busy to have lunch at the moment."

The car ride is quicker than I thought, and I am excited to see my baby. I can't wait to wrap my arms around him and love on him. This man is one that I have prayed for and now, I finally have him. The only thing keeping me from him is the woman he doesn't want anymore. Why should I suffer because the woman won't let go?

I walk into his building right past his receptionist who has an uh oh look on her face, but I don't care about anything they have going on here. Hell, this is his business and I won't be taking part in this shit when he takes it from his wife. My heart freezes over at the sight that stood before me, stopping me in my tracks. I know this shit can't be happening.

The sight of Markus kissing his wife makes my blood boil hotter than the center of the earth. This is some bullshit, and I'm going to make sure he leaves her sooner rather than later. I pull out my phone and fire off a text.

Lynn: I can't believe you are kissing her and you knew I was coming here on your lunch break. What the fuck are you thinking?

I see him looking at his phone when the message goes through. The look of shock on his face is priceless as he scans around his office to try and find me. Our eyes meet through the window, but he quickly returns his attention to his wife.

Lynn: So you're going to stand there and ignore me? I hope you know I'm not going to be left alone tonight so you better get that shit out of your system.

I look up at him and again he is wrapped up in her, kissing her in a way he has never kissed me. I can tell there is so much passion in the way she kisses, looks, and hugs him. She loves him, I love him too, and I'm not going to lose him. I will do anything to make sure I keep the man I love even if that means making his little wife disappear.

I watch them for a second longer, letting it fuel my anger and hatred for the woman to set my plan into action. I shake my head when Julian looks at me right before knocking on Markus' office door, waiting for him to let him in. This has got to end and soon. I walked away and almost let my tears fall, but I wouldn't give that bitch the satisfaction.

I sat in the living room waiting on this man and to hear the stupid explanation he is going to come up with about what happened. I know it's going to be stupid because what can he say to make me feel like his display of affection with her is justified? The headlights of his car shine through the window, and I brace myself for the shit storm that's about to start.

The door opens and his eyes look like he has been on one all day. "What the fuck is wrong with you?" Markus asks, not taking a second to speak.

"What do you mean what's wrong with me? What the fuck is wrong with you? You had that bitch in your office hugging and kissing you and you knew I was coming to have lunch with you. I thought you didn't love her anymore!" I yell at him.

"That's my wife so her being in my office is her right, hell the shit is half hers anyway, and whatever I do with my wife is my business. You act like I'm cheating on you. You are the other woman and you need to know your place until that shit changes." He returns the raised tone in his voice.

I watch him take off his jacket, walks into the room, and lie across the bed, "So I'm not supposed to be mad at the fact that you were kissing a woman that's not supposed to matter?"

"No, because you knew what it was from the start and you just have to wait until this shit takes shape if you want any chance of being the next Mrs."

I'm so mad at him that it makes my head hurt to even continue to think about it. I know I have to do something because I can't risk losing him and with the attitude he's presenting, I may be in danger considering he is defending her where he usually is bashing her and talking shit to her.

He gets up and walks into the bathroom, leaving his phone on the bed. I hurry and snatch it up, keeping my ears at attention for when he is finished using it. I type in his code and scroll through his call log and find the name Bae in his phone, and I know that has to be me. So, I keep scrolling and notice my number there without a name on it.

"My number ain't even saved in his phone," I whisper to myself. The toilet flushes, and I know it's only a matter of a few seconds before he walks back into the room. The sink faucet starts, and I scroll back up to Bae and tap the arrow to get the details. I write down the number and place the phone back on the bed as the sound of the water from the sink shuts off. This bitch has it all, even though he doesn't love he still saves her as his "bae". I have to do something, and this isn't going to be as easy as I thought.

*****

The wind blowing against my face makes me start to cool down considering I have been heated for the last few days. I just can't believe that number one, Markus talked to me like that and number two, that he still loves her after he made me believe that there was nothing there for him anymore.

"What's wrong? Are you still thinking about what happened with your man?" Brandi asks.

Brandi is another friend that worked with us at the warehouse, but she ended up leaving after she got her new job working for a new local car manufacturing company. She is a little older, but she has been on my side with this shit. Hell, she has even gone as far as to fuck with his friend to keep in contact and do little shit to keep shit going with Markus and his wife. Hell, when she first told me about her being on the phone with him, and she knew he was with his wife from hearing her in the background she goes on to mention him being with me. She told me he ended the call only to call her back later to cuss her out about fucking with his life at home. I thought the shit was hilarious, and he ended up in my bed that night so I guess she did a good job.

"Yeah, I think I have to take matters into my own hands to get him to leave his wife. I mean I have her number even though I don't know what I'm going to do with it yet."

At that moment, Markus pulls into the driveway, gets out of the car, and speaking to everybody. Without another glance at him, I get up and walk into the house. This is going to be the perfect chance for her to see that she's not wanted anymore and she can let him go. I start to pull up his wife's number and call her but removing it from the display.

I walk into the kitchen and grab a beer from the refrigerator and stand there, waiting on Markus to enter the kitchen.

"What's your problem?" he asks, leaning against me. "If you're going to have this attitude then I'm going to leave. I can go home if I want to deal with somebody's attitude."

I hear the low sound of his wife's voice coming from the phone. "Well if you wouldn't do things to hurt me then we wouldn't have these problems. Since you're talking shit you can go home to your wife."

"She's not my wife. We only put that shit on paper for a certain situation and it was only for that. I keep telling you we are not married."

I can see him getting frustrated. "Well you seemed to like it was something different the other day when you were so gung-ho to defend her. Make that shit make sense."

"I don't want to talk about this," Markus says.

He starts to kiss me pulling my pants down and lifting me to sit on the counter. "You sure you gonna fuck me on the counter?"'

"Why does it matter where I fuck you? It's my pussy, right?"

"Yeah, it's yours and it could be yours all the time if you move in and stop playing this back and forth game." I let out a gasp as he sinks his dick inside me. I look down at my phone to see the green bubble in the top left corner letting me know his wife is still on the phone.

"Um huh, stop talking that shit and take this dick," Markus says with his strokes constant and deep.

The green bubble disappears from the phone, and Brandi walks into the kitchen, "Oh my bad, I just needed to get another beer," she said, turning away from us.

"It's fine, I think I made my point," I said, pushing him back and hopping off the counter. I pull my pants back up and walk back outside with my beer in my hand.

"What's that supposed to mean?" Markus asks. I keep walking as if I didn't hear him.

Now, all we have to do is wait. After that little show, she should be packing his shit right now and waiting for him to get there so she can put him out and send him home where he belongs.

*****

It's been two days, and I haven't heard from or seen Markus at all. This is some actual bullshit. What the fuck do I have to do to get her to leave him? For the hundredth time, I send him a message.

Me: So you are playing the perfect husband right now, huh? What kind of game do you think you are playing with me? The games need to end now because I'm pregnant again and I'm not getting rid of it this time so don't fuckin' say shit about it. It's time for you to get

your shit together and come home. You don't even love her so fuck what you have left and just end this bullshit marriage.

I know he's not going to answer so it's time to go to the next best thing. I call his wife and listen to the phone ring with my palms starting to sweat. "Hello." Her voice almost sounds sweet, but I don't know if that's because she doesn't remember my number or what.

"I know this isn't your problem, but I need you to tell Markus he needs to come home so he can check in with the mother of his child," I say my voice almost in a tremble.

"Wait, what are you talking about? Markus doesn't know that I'm pregnant so what do you mean?"

Hearing her say she's pregnant makes me want to reach through the phone and snatch the baby right out of her womb. "No, I can give two fucks about your baby. I'm pregnant with his baby, and he needs to come home to tend to me knowing this is going to be hard for me to endure."

The line goes quiet until I hear them arguing and Markus begging and making every excuse in the book about me lying. This has to be the end. Hell, she's pregnant and finds out she's pregnant at the same time as the real love of his life has to break her down in a way that should destroy her soul. "I have finally won," I say into the phone before hanging up, leaving them to finish their argument.

Ember

I can't believe this is what I have to endure to keep what is supposed to already belong to me. This man is making me question if it's worth it to try and make this shit work. What did I do in a past life to deserve this shit? I mean damn how much does a bitch have to take to make a man understand the love I have for him is real? I have to get out of this relationship. I can't stay here anymore and give him what I think he is entitled to. That's about the only reason I can think of he could be doing this to me. I don't waste any time getting my ass back on the phone with this divorce lawyer.

"Good morning, This is Ember Ballard, and I know it's been a few weeks since we last spoke, but unfortunately, I'm back I would like to go over my options again." I can feel the lump growing in my throat again. I know this is what I need to do to free myself no matter how painful it is.

"It's nice to hear from you again. I wish it was under different circumstances. We can sit down and meet today around three if you would like?" the deep voice of the divorce attorney says through the phone. I don't know if he's flirting with me or just being nice.

"Three is perfect. Thank you and I will see you then." My heart is racing but not because of the divorce anymore. Maybe I can be friends with the man behind the deep voice.

Trying to relax is harder than it looks. The million thoughts running through my head right now isn't making it all that easy. While watching my ceiling fan circle the room, I can't help but wonder how I'm going to feel at the end of all this.

The slamming of the front door brings my thoughts to a screeching halt, and Markus flies into the room as if he conquered the stairs in a single bound. Confusion and fear fill me, wondering what the hell is wrong with this man.

"Baby, do you have any extra cash on you? The bank isn't open, and I can't find my debit card," Markus said panicked, sweaty, and out of breath.

I look at him, but I can't believe the words coming out of his mouth. "So you're telling me that again you have lost your debit card?" I asked, giving him air quotes for lost.

"Babe, I don't have time right now. I promise you can bitch at me later. I just need this right now. Do you have anything on you right now?"

"Yes, I think I have about two hundred dollars in my purse. What do you need it for?" I ask, waiting for him to hand me my purse.

"We have a homeboy that's in some trouble and we are all pitching in to help him," Markus explains.

"Who the fuck is your homeboy and who the fuck are *we* you are referring to?"

"I can't do this right now Em. Can you give it to me or not?" I hand him the two hundred dollars, but I already know he's lying.

I lay back on the bed and start watching TV but stop listening to the bullshit spewing from his lying lips. He stands in front of the TV.

"Can you please move?"

"So you're just going to sit there and pretend like you don't hear me talking to you?"

"I don't care about you getting all big in the chest and calling yourself getting mad at me. I'm tired of all your half-truths and shit so you got it. I don't care anymore." This shit can't be over fast enough for me.

"Fine, I'll be back later."

After rolling my eyes so much they hurt, I lay back again and watch TV. Nothing is going to change with this man, and I have come to accept it.

The trip to see this attorney is much needed considering it's like a small breath of fresh air. I mean I can feel the weight slowly being removed from me. I just have to follow through and not let him get into my head. This man knows I love him and being without him used to be the last thing I would want in this world.

"Hi, my name is Ember Ballard and I'm here to see Mr. Kraig Morton," I say to his receptionist sitting at the desk.

"I'll let him know you're here. Please have a seat over there, and he'll be out when he's ready," the woman says, picking up the phone. I nod and take my seat while listening to her make the call. "Mr. Morton, your three o'clock is here. Yes, sir."

The ticking of the clock puts my senses on a heightened alert, the smell of the office becomes more and more intense, and the sound of my heart starts to drown out everything around me. I feel my head start to swim and get dizzy.

"Mrs. Ballard, good afternoon. You can come back to my office," the familiar deep voice says from next to the receptionist's desk.

This man is more handsome than I thought. His light green eyes are surrounded by his peanut butter skin tone and full black beard. His smile is amazing and reveals his perfect white smile from behind his full, juicy lips. I give him a onceover and his chest and stomach outline his white button down collared shirt perfectly and his pants…let's just say I don't need to use my imagination much to know the man is blessed.

I stand from my chair and follow him to his office; his smooth stride makes it hard to stay focused on the task at hand. "Thank you for seeing me today," I say as he steps aside to let me enter his office.

"It's my pleasure. Now can you tell me a little about your marriage and what led down the road to divorce?" I swear the look in his eye makes me almost fall into a trance or under his spell.

"First, we have been together for seven years and this is not the first time he has cheated," I explain, feeling my bones start to hurt from all the buried pain inside of me. "I forgave him and let him back in, but then he started this up again and I just can't let myself go through it. I love my husband with everything in me, but what's the point of fighting an uphill battle when you are the only one fighting?" The warm tears roll down my cheeks and attempting to blink any new ones away is not working.

"I understand, and I apologize for everything you have had to go through. I have to ask do you have proof of his infidelity?" Mr. Morton asks. I can see the sympathy in his eyes as he hands me a Kleenex.

"Yes, I have an old camera of videos of him having sex with this woman. It has the time and date stamped on it. I can bring that to you."

"You can tell it's him in the video?"

"Yes, he is in full view and when I confronted him he just looked at me like I was crazy." He doesn't care, and I can't let this keep happening to me. He does not take into consideration the pain he is causing me. He doesn't care that he doesn't have any respect for me or our relationship." Another wave of tears covers my face as I frantically try to wipe them away.

"Mrs. Ballard, I hope this is not being too forward or inappropriate, but you are too beautiful of a woman to be crying like this over a man that doesn't care to realize the diamond he has in his hand. I will take your case, but you can't waiver from this. I am going to take him for everything he owes you. Do you have any assets together?"

I can look at him and tell he is wanting to help me, and it's coming from a good place. I just want to keep this moving without any hiccups. I want to be freed from all this, and I don't want to be a victim of this anymore. The rest of the conversation plays out better than expected and only takes an hour and a half. As I leave this office, I feel better as my soul has gotten a really good cleaning. It's not all gone yet, but I can feel it being washed away little by little. This is just the beginning of being the free woman I have desired to be for the past year.

*****

I have to be careful how I move. I have to keep this to myself until I get the ball rolling. I walk through the office, beckoning Mya and Shae to a sit down with me in my office. I need a little girls' time since I have had myself locked away the last few days, and I need something else to occupy my mind besides my pending divorce. I sit down watching them file in like a swarm of ants going on a hike to the nearest ionic basket.

"Ok, ladies," I say as they take their seats across from me. "There is something I need to talk to you about. I need to take my mind off of the shit that's going on around me. So who's going first to make my day a brighter one?" I ask, clapping my hands together.

"Well, I can tell you what happened to me last night," Mya starts. "Lance attempted to make us a candle lit dinner last night. He had the table all set up in the dining room with the wine in the bucket of ice, music playing low and slow, the smell of the food was a nice touch," she says then she rolls her eyes.

"Ok, so what happened? How can you go wrong with that?" Shae asks.

"He end up trying to start some shit, and I told him he needed to go check on the food before he tried to take me down but he didn't listen. So, he saw a flame ignite on the stove and he got up with his pants around his ankles to run to the kitchen. Y'all when I say he fell, I mean he slid across the dining room floor into the bucket of ice. Then, while he was trying to get up he was constantly falling back to the floor. I could not help but kill over laughing. I was laughing so hard I couldn't get up to go put the fire out. Luckily though, he had installed the little shower or sprinkler thing on the hood of the stove for such instances."

Listening to them all laugh makes me happy that someone in my life is able to feel some form of joy and peace no matter what minor issues they have on the side. The ringing of my phone stops everyone in the room from talking given that I just let it ring and go to voicemail then start over again.

"Um, Ember sweetie, that's the fourth time your phone has rang. Whoever that is wants to talk to you."

I snatch up the phone. "What?"

"Why didn't you answer the phone the first time? I don't want to be waiting on you to answer the phone every time I call. Em, stop fuckin' playin' with me."

I hang up, slamming the phone on my desk. Hell, I thought I had broken it, but that's wishful thinking cause the stupid ass phone starts to ring again. This time Shae grabs the phone. "I'm sorry, but Mrs. Ballard is busy with clients right now can I take a message," she said in her most professional voice.

I can tell his ass is getting pissed off by the tone of his voice. To be honest, it sounded kind of sexy. "No, you can put her ass on the phone. Who is this? Kacey, the new girl? Do you know I'm your boss too, right, and I can fire you? Now put my wife on the phone."

What the fuck am I thinking? Stay focused, bitch. We got this. I can't be getting hung up on his little ploys to try and suck me back in.

"No, this is not Kacey, sir, but I will be happy to tell her you called. Thank you for calling." She hurriedly pushes the end button on the phone, smirking and looking around at us. "I'm sorry. I didn't mean to overstep, but I can tell you are tired and need a minute to collect yourself," she says.

"It's fine. His ass is just doing the absolute most right now, and he knows he can kind of suck me back in with his aggressiveness. So, I'm trying my damnedest not to let him see that right now. I have to keep my eye on the prize."

"So have you decided what you're going to do? I mean no one can make the choice but you and no one is living it but you. So, whatever you decide you will have our support," Mya says, sympathetically.

She has had her own experience with a divorce that I recently came to find out during one of our little girl talks. It took a lot for her to be done with the marriage. She tells me all the time she understands being caught between wanting to leave due to being taken for granted and disrespected but wanting to stay because it's the man I fell in love with and want to spend my life with.

"Yes and no. I have started talking to a divorce attorney, and he's ready to take the case. He also warned me that once he gets started there won't be no turning back. I mean I can't blame him, so that's why I haven't told him yes or no yet. I love my husband, but if the shoe was on the other foot he would be in jail awaiting trial for my murder," I explain with a lump the size of Texas in my throat. "I don't want to lose my husband, but I can't do this cheating shit anymore. I can't keep being a choice. I want to be the only one just like he's that for me. Am I wrong for wanting that?" I ask, sincerely looking for an answer.

Everybody looks awkward and as if the tension weighed a few tons pushing down on us all. "Look this is where you are just…" Mya starts to say.

"We don't need to talk about this. We need to worry about getting these new clients under our thumb. I mean I know we have met our quota, but if we can secure the bag with a couple of more companies then we can hire maybe one or two more people. I just need this to keep us afloat and all hands be on deck."

"You got it. I think we can make it happen with just us and that way we can get bigger bonuses this year for the holidays." Shae rubs her hands together with a devilish look on her face.

The rest of the day has been uneventful which didn't bother me one bit. At least I had the rest of the day to relax and get my mind to work through some of the bullshit. The house doesn't feel like a home anymore. It doesn't have the vibe that we built this together in it anymore and that breaks my heart every time I step foot in here.

While taking in the room and all the pictures of our memories on the wall, I know the man I married is still in there somewhere I just don't think I can wait for him to decide to come back to me.

Sighing and walking up the stairs, I say, "This too shall pass." The loud ringing of my phone startles me, and I almost rolled my butt back down the stairs. I grab my chest with my heart racing inside it.

"Hello." I hurriedly push the accept and answer.

"Hey, Ember, I haven't heard from you in a while. Where have you been?" Marie asks. Marie is Markus' sister and since we officially met, we had gotten kind of close. She is sweet, but I have gotten little glimpses of how ruthless she can be with people she doesn't have the patience to fuck with or that has crossed her. Overall though, she's a good person to have on your team.

"No, I've been around. Hell trying to make sure we keep this business on top. How about you? What have you been getting into? Wait let me guess, you have a new boo?" I ask with half chuckle.

"Girl, I have to tell you about it. You want to go out for a drink?"

I think about the day I've had and then the last few weeks. "Yea we can go. I'll meet you there."

Illusions is her spot and nobody can convince her to go anywhere else. I think she may have tried to hit up Deja Vu's once before, but it was something about their drinks she didn't like so Illusions it is.

The clothes inside my closet seem to form a tunnel as I look around to try and find something to wear. I want to wear a dress, but not too short. Hell, it would be just my luck if Markus walked his red ass in there and sees us hanging out.

That man thinks we aren't supposed to go anywhere that has any other men in attendance without him. Like he's somebody's daddy or something.

This dark forest green, deep cowl neck, backless dress will get the job done. Oh yes with the black pumps, we will be the talk of the club tonight. A quick shower and into the night we will go.

It doesn't take long for me to spot her at the bar already getting the bartender to hand her a shot. "I see you started without me." I tap Marie on the shoulder.

"You know I had to." She gave the bartender a seductive grin. I shake my head at her but laugh. "What? He knows what's up."

"Anyway so tell me about this new guy."

"Oh, so I met him on this dating site. He's cute and he's from the town."

"Ok so have you gone out on a date yet?"

"No, but he has sent me some money for me to get something to wear to take some pictures in for him. Here, this him." She turns her phone toward me to show me a picture of a man around our age. He looks alright, but he doesn't look like he's her type. Then again, I may be wrong. I mean he's cashin' out without getting any suga.

"Really?" I say, feeling my face kind of twist a little.

"What's wrong with him?"

"Nothing."

"It doesn't matter because he's here today and will be gone tomorrow if he breathes wrong."

I laugh and scan around to see all the faces in the crowd, but I know even entertaining a glance would not be the thing to do right now. The music play as I sway my hips to the beat a little bit, and I'm starting to feel the music. "What are you drinking? I need one after the day I've had today."

"I'm drinking 1800 mango." She waves her hand at the bartender making drinks at the other end of the bar.

The night went by in a blur, but I know I got two guys kicked out of the club last night. I think my dress did its job a little too well. With a splitting headache, I lay there looking at the sun peeking through the edge of the curtains.

"Hey, do you have any aspirin?" Marie asks, leaning against the threshold of the door.

"Yea, go look behind the mirror in my bathroom." I wave my hand toward the other door.

"You know I got that dude's number for you. I don't know why you keep calling my brother your husband. It's not like y'all are married, right?"

"What makes you think we aren't married?"

"Because he told me y'all aren't married like had a wedding or anything."

"No, we didn't have a wedding, but that's my husband. We are married, well I thought we were, but I guess I didn't get the memo."

"That's something I will not do and that's claim and man that doesn't claim me. To be for real, I wouldn't claim him even if he claimed me until I have papers in hand on his ass," she calls from the bathroom.

"Well I don't want to talk to that guy. Are we still going to lunch at the new seafood restaurant on the expressway?" I ask, changing the subject.

I hate knowing about all the negative things Markus has said about me and our relationship. It seems that everybody knows we aren't married except for me. I wish he would have told me, and I wouldn't be walking around here embarrassing myself.

"Yeah, but it's still early. I need a nap."

"It's ten minutes after one." I laugh at her, pulling the covers back up to my nose. Hell, a nap doesn't sound half-bad at the moment.

"Oh shit, I need to go to that house. We can have lunch tomorrow after this hangover is gone, and I can think straight."

She leaves, and I hear the front door open and close before snuggling back into my bed and blanket. I notice for the first time I am completely naked.

*****

Walking to the bathroom seems to get more difficult with the room spinning, but it has slowed a little since the last bathroom trip. Jumping at the sound of the door, I brace myself for Markus to walk through the door as I make my way back to the bed holding my head in my hands.

"Did you have fun with my sister last night?" he asks, walking over to the bed.

"Please not now. I have a headache." I pull the covers back on the bed.

"So who the fuck was that who was at the table with y'all? Don't lie, Em," he asks. I look at him while not being able to focus on his face. "You don't hear me talking to you now?"

"I hear you, but I'm trying to figure out who the fuck you're talking about."

He shoves me onto the bed. I feel everything in my stomach want to come up, but I hold it in, closing my eyes and trying to keep it together. "Wait, why the hell were you following and spying on me?"

The burn and the echo of the slap across my face fill the room. "You must think I'm stupid or something. Do you think I need you? I can make it without you. I don't need anything from you and to be honest, you have been holding me back."

He disappears into the closet, and I hold my face still in shock that this man put his hands on me. This man that promised to protect me has raised his hand to harm me. I feel the tears coming, but then he returns holding his duffel bag and starts to pull clothes from his drawer.

I watched him closely and with every piece of clothing placed into the bag, I feel a little lighter. My emotions run through me a million miles a minute with every one of them surfacing and wanting to explode through, but the shock just won't let go of me. He shoots me a murderous glance as he makes his way around the room, not uttering a word.

"Thank you for making this easy for me. I never thought you would do this to me but thank you," I finally say as he's walking out the door. He doesn't turn back to look at me or say anything. He only stops for a second before leaving the house.

This is not the way I want my marriage to end, but this is the end. I put up with a lot of shit. Hitting me is a deal breaker for me, and there's no coming back from it.

Markus

The night before replays itself in my head repeatedly as the pain in my baby's eyes turns to anger. I don't know how she managed to stay so calm, but after hearing her voice and the emotionless tone, I couldn't bear to turn around. I couldn't look at the damage I caused with my stupidity and irrational thinking. The night seems surreal just lying there looking at the ceiling of Aaron's guestroom. I couldn't and still can't believe I had done that to the woman I love. She is my everything and then I had the nerve to tell her I didn't need her. She is the backbone of everything we have and although I can make it without her it's going to be hard as hell and it won't feel the same. I need that woman, but my pride just won't let me call her to apologize.

"So, are you going just lay in the bed all day and sulk?" Aaron asks, popping his head through the door.

"I don't know what the fuck I was thinking. I know this is the end of my marriage. After that shit last night, Ember won't be taking me back. I have put her through so much shit and I keep adding shit to make her not trust me.. I know she's done."

"What the hell did you do?" Aaron walks completely into the room with a sour look on his face.

"I put my hands on her," I say almost in a whisper.

"You did what?"

"I hit her. I slapped her."

"What the fuck, man? How could you put your hands on that

woman? You are going to regret that shit for the rest of your life."

"I just hope she doesn't call the police on me."

"She's not going to do that and if you were fucked-up and wanted that woman, you wouldn't be the shit that you do to her." Aaron's voice is overflowing with disappointment.

"I do want my wife, and I love her. I don't know what the fuck is wrong with me. I just can't help myself sometimes."

"If you want to be with her then you need to do what it takes to get her back and work that shit out because I can tell you one thing for sure, you won't find another woman like her. You will compare and try to mold everybody coming after her to be like her, but they won't be able to hold a candle to her on their best day," Aaron scolds me.

I can't say he's wrong or he's lying. He has been here for most of the relationship, and he knows the shit that I've done. I've watched her break right before my eyes, and with a smile say she's fine. I have felt the pain that comes with the fucked-up shit that I do and yet, I still continue to do stupid shit. I guess it's just a matter of watching and waiting to see what happens next.

*****

My days are running together, and I don't know which way is up, but I have picked up the phone a thousand times ready to apologize. There is something not letting me do it. I don't know if it's because I know I'm not going to stop or if it's because I know she's not going to take me back. I can't even lie and say I can feel a little bit of her presence in me anymore. I know she's gone, and there is nothing I can do about it.

I lay my head on my desk, letting the pity flow through me. "You have a call on line three," Julian says at the door.

"Alright, thank you." I grab the phone. "This is Markus Ballard, how can I help you?" I ask.

"I was told you needed to speak with me." The sweet angelic voice of my baby lifts me. Excitement is bursting through, me and I almost yelp out loud.

"Um, yeah. I want to see if we can meet for lunch so we can talk if that's alright." I clear my throat.

"I don't know if I can do that right now," Ember says on the other end of the phone. Her rejection breaks my heart, but what should I expect?

"Em, baby, please. I just need a few minutes of your time. Please." The silence lasts a few seconds, but it feels like hours. "I know this is something you don't want to do, but please just give me a few minutes. We will be in a public place."

"Fine. We can meet at Coffee and Cake," she says. I feel the hesitation down to my bones as she speaks. "I will only be able to stay during my lunch break."

"Ok, Will twelve fifteen be alright with you? "

"Yes, please don't be late. I have a lot going on here."

I count down the few hours I have until I try and fight for my marriage. I just hope she gives me a chance to make my point and apologize to her.

I sat down in the coffee shop five minutes early, waiting to see Ember walking down the sidewalk. I prepare myself for whatever she might say including rejection, but I don't want to be without my wife. I want to go back home and be secure and know the woman I wake up to every morning is the one that is going to always have my back as she has done for the last seven years.

Finally arriving, I see her step into view walking with her head held high and confident. She looks so pure and loving, but I still see the pain in her eyes. As she walks through the door, she gives me a half-smile. I guess it was a good idea to sit in the corner next to the counter.

I stand to greet her. "Hey babe, can I get you anything?" I wrap my arms around her, embracing her. Her body feels so good against mine. This is home, and I want this back.

"Um…yea. I'll take a caramel cappuccino," she says, sitting with her back to the wall.

After returning to the counter and placing the order, I get excited to talk to her so I make haste getting back to the table. "I want to say, first I'm sorry for everything that has happened. I should have never put my hands on you, and I should have listened to you instead of pushing what you needed aside." I take her hands in mine.

"I don't want you to say all this because you think this is what I want to hear. I want you to do what you are saying. I need you to make me feel safe the way you used to because right now, I don't feel safe with you and I don't trust you at all. You used to be my everything and nothing or no one could take that away from you. I wanted that back, but it's like you didn't want it and you found what you wanted in the streets, and I was just your comfort spot and you knew I wouldn't leave you."

"Baby, I know and I promise I'm going to work on that. I mean it's not going to happen overnight, but I'm going to bust my ass every day to do this right. Just please let me come back home. I love you with all my heart, and I don't want anyone else."

She gives me a sideways look and tries to hide her smile, but I know this is going to end well. I can see her coming back to me, but I see her hiding her pain and anger from me.

"I don't know if this is going to work. I don't want to feel like I'm spinning my wheels. Maybe I shouldn't expect anything from you. I mean look at us. Look at the lives we are living right now. This is never what I thought it would be being married to you. I love you, and I can't say I feel that coming from you."

Guilt resurfaces and the optimism starts to fade, "I don't want to rush you to choose, but I heard you and everything I said I meant. I want you to be comfortable and know that you are making the right choice. I love you." I kiss the back of her hand and leave her sitting at the table alone.

I can't stand to look at her, knowing I can't come home to her. I don't want to think about all the shit that she may be doing especially with her friend, Mya. The crisp wind blows against my face, cooling me down from being so upset. The piercing screeching of tires makes me turn back toward the coffee shop to see a car speeding in my direction. I look into the car, but I can't tell who is behind the wheel. Running back to help, I see a crowd of people forming around whoever was involved in the incident.

Making my way to the front of the crowd, I see it's Ember laying on the ground holding her right leg.

"Em, what happened?" I ask, panic coursing through me. I don't know what I'm going to do if something happens to her.

"That car tried to hit me and pinned my leg between these cars. I can't move. Please, Markus help me," she begs with tears covering her face.

"I got you." I glanced at the man standing over us calling 9-1-1. "I'm right here, baby, and I'm not going anywhere."

I sat in the waiting room as everything goes through my mind. Who could have done this and why? Everybody loves Em and either use her or needs her in their lives. People are drawn to her like a moth to a flame and cutting her off is impossible; being without her, you will notice. The vibe in everyday life will not be the same in any aspect.

Mya and Shae walk into the hospital door with worry and fear written on their faces. "Please tell me she's alright," Mya ask with tears filling her eye.

"I don't know. We met at Coffee and Cake and when I left, she was still in the coffee shop, but I heard the car's tires and when I turned around, I saw people huddling around her. I went back, and she was laying on the ground between two cars on the street. She told me that the car that hit her pinned her leg between another car," I explain to them both.

"So, why aren't you back there with her?"

"She's in surgery." I sat down in my seat. It's my fault she's even going through this. It's my fault she was there, and I will die if something major is going wrong with her. Em is the love of my life and this shit is not worth it.

We all pace the floor, waiting when the surgeon walks into the waiting room. "Ballard family."

*****

Watching my baby sleep gives me a sense of relief, but it kills me to know when she's not sleeping she's in pain. Wrapping my arms around her waist, I slide as close to her as possible and push my face into her hair. Her scent turns me on, but I lay next to her with my eyes closed, just happy to be home.

"Wake up." Em's voice is soft and a little scratchy but still as angelic as ever.

"How are you feeling?" I know the pain had to be returning since it's passed the time for her to take her next dosage of medicine. It's crazy her leg is broken in three places and now she has to deal with having a rod in her leg for the rest of her life.

"I'm in a little pain, but I want to deal with it for as long as possible. I don't want to get used to taking all that stuff," she says. Her face twists with pain as she turns to adjust to the bed. For six weeks, this is what I'm gonna have to do. I have to make sure I can take care of my baby, and this may be the only time I will have to show her I meant what I said about changing.

"I will leave everything here next to the bed, and Mya is supposed to come over in about fifteen minutes. Do you need to do anything before I leave for work?" I ask before getting out of bed with her.

"No, have a good day, and don't spend all day worrying about me, alright." A big smile stretched across her face before kissing me passionately. I have missed this so much it hurts but with the fire and desire that she has always given me. It's time to get it back.

"Alright, baby. I love you and take care of yourself, ok."

Leaving is the hardest thing I have had to do lately. I don't want to leave her for someone else to take care of. I know Mya is going to make sure she's alright, but it's nothing like knowing that it's getting done right.

It feels different walking into work with the weight of Em holding me down. This shit is eating me alive knowing it's my fault she is laying there hurt and in pain. I stop in my tracks when I see Lynn standing there, waiting for me with her arms crossed and a pissed off look on her face.

"I don't have time for this today. I have so much on my plate right now and listening to you bitch about whatever it is you are here for."

"Well, you're going to make time. I saw you with that bitch. How the fuck do you keep telling me that you want to be with me and you're only using her to get what you need. Then, on the other hand, you are all kissing one her and shit like that's where you want to be. I haven't heard from you in two weeks and you think this is going to go unpunished?"

Lynn yells, getting the attention of everyone in the building.

"Like I said I don't have time for your shit right now. I have a lot on my plate and taking care of my wife is my main priority right now." I step around her, leaving her in the lobby.

"'You think this is the end? Well, this shit just started. Mark my words, you and your little wife are gonna pay for playing with me."

I can't get to this office fast enough to close the door behind me. I don't want to deal with her shit right now. My computer is open to all my business contacts and properties. The feeling of anger and fear occupy my whole body.

"Julian, I need to see you in my office as soon as possible," I call his extension.

"What's up, Markie boy." Julian burst through the office door.

"Who has been in my office? All of my files are open, and I know I didn't have this pulled up when I went home," I explain to him.

"Oh, that was me. I needed to find the previous selling price on one of the Riverdale Ave. properties. The owner is wanting to sell because of some money issues and needing to downsize." Julian erases my fear.

"You could have at least closed it all out. Did you find what you needed? I knew that property was going to be a problem for them. It's a lot of money for the upkeep and then buying the house itself."

"Well, I put the house on the market for double what they bought it for because they made some nice upgrades to the whole property. I think it could have gone for more, but they want it sold as quickly as possible."

I click on the property and look at the newly added pictures to see the upgrades made to the house. This house is going for way less than the market price. "I think I may have a buyer for this house, and they will continue with the renovations and upgrading. It is going to make the property value of the houses around it go up as well so we have to make sure we consider that when and if they are back on the market."

After he leaves, I look at all the newly added properties that have been put up for either rental or sale. They have been busy since I've been gone, but I can't say that I'm complaining though. This is going to bring in a lot of money all around. I make the best of it all and get to calling around to the buyers I know are ready to buy, and don't let the bumps of the morning drag this day down.

The laughter coming from upstairs makes my heart smile. I know my baby is feeling better. Well enough to be laughing and cutting up with Mya. I smile as I walk into the bedroom and look at them sitting in the middle of the bed with snacks spread around them. Em has her leg propped up on the throw pillows to support it.

"Well it's been fun, but I'm gonna let you two love birds have it," Mya says, gathering her things and putting on her shoes.

"Thank you, Mya, for staying with my baby." I lean down and kiss Em on the forehead. "How are you feeling, baby?"

"I'm alright. I had to finally give in and take the meds. It got way too unbearable. Thank you, Mya."

"It's all good, and I'll see you tomorrow. Don't let David get you in trouble with his shenanigans. Oh and make sure he finishes getting the truck information sent to you. I have already got truck numbers for a few of them," Mya says, waving as she leaves the bedroom. I would be fooling no one but myself if I say that didn't just piss me off.

"Who is David and what is he going to do to get you into trouble?" I ask, trying to keep my tone even.

"Oh, he's the son of the guy, Gavin, I sent to you about buying some property. You know they have a trucking company and they are adding trucks to their fleet. He is dragging his feet on getting us all the information, but when he is communicating with us he's playing and telling jokes."

"Oh, I thought this was the guy from the club you were at the table with when you were with my sister," I replied.

"No, I told you I didn't want anything to do with that situation at all. That was not my doing."

"Alright, you're going to listen to me one day," I say, shaking my head and undressing. I feel her eyes on my back, but I'm not going to turn around. My baby be dick watching, and I just want to see the look on her face when I turn around and I'm naked.

Without another thought, I turn and walk to the bathroom glancing over at her. "What are you looking at me like that for?" I ask.

"Nothing." The smile was even wider than before.

"I know that look. Wait until I get out of the shower and I got you, but we have to be careful," I tell her, shooting her a little wink. My baby is just as goofy and crazy as I am.

Our night is something out of a romance movie. We made love like it was the first time. We didn't let the tensions of the last few weeks get in the way of what we felt for one another. That woman knows just how to make me feel loved. I can't believe I was about to lose it all over something that doesn't even compete with what I have right in front of me.

I roll over to see my beauty sleeping peacefully, and the flickering light from the TV lights up the tears that have settled in the corner of her eye. I wipe the tear, and I watch her wince from the pain of trying to move and adjust. I don't know if I can say that it's really from the pain or the pain that I have caused her. She doesn't deserve the shit I do, and I know damn well I don't deserve her. I just hope I don't let her down. Wrapping my arms around her, I pull her to my chest and kiss her on top of her head. This is going to be harder than I thought it was going to be.

*****

The day is one of the best we have had in the company all year. We have properties being sold left and right, and the rental properties are being occupied even faster. This is going to be the reason I have to give out bonuses for the New Year. I almost forgot the New Year's Eve party is in three days. I didn't even get my wife anything for Christmas. With her being hurt, we stayed in bed all day on Christmas.

"Hey, you want to head to lunch with us? I think we might be getting some sushi at the new sushi spot in the square." Julian peeks his head into my office door.

"Yea, let me grab my jacket and keys and I'll meet you in the lobby," I say, wrapping up the email I have been working on for the last thirty minutes. This is what I need Em for. She knows just what to say no matter what business she is running for us. I used to say she's the brain and I'm the muscle behind everything. I think she is a mixture of both, and I'm just here to help pull it all together.

The lobby doors open, letting a crisp breeze blowing in and along with it. Lynn stands there with two bags of food and drinks. Julian gives me an 'oh damn' look when they all realize who she is.

"I'll catch the next lunch outing," I say and wave everyone off.

"I can go let you go out to lunch with everybody," Lynn says, and I know damn well she doesn't want that in the least bit. That woman always wants her way.

"Nah, you're here now. So come on. We can eat in the conference room. My desk is full of work documents," I say, leading the way to the conference room with my hand on the small of her back. "So what are we having?"

"I got us a couple of BBQ burgers," she says, stepping into the room and relieving the bags on the table.

We sit down and start eating without saying anything, but I can tell there is something on her mind that she is waiting to get off. I wipe the barbecue sauce from my mouth and lean back in the chair waiting for her to speak. She doesn't say anything, prompting me to call and check on Em. The line rings and rings with no answer until it goes to her voicemail.

"I know she is with that nigga, and I know it's more than what they are saying he is with her," I say just above a whisper.

'Why do you care? You all stressed and pressed over someone you are only supposed to using to get what you want?" Lynn asks, clearly upset.

"You know she is my wife, right?"

"According to you, she's not your wife so which is it?"

"Look, you knew what this shit was before you got into it so don't start with this bullshit like I'm just your man or something."

"You are my man and the only man I happen to be fuckin' right now for your information."

"Let's go for a ride," I say, standing and throwing my wrappers into the empty bag.

"For what?"

"Get your ass up and let's go," I demand.

We pile into her car and it's funny that I've seen this car before. I just can't put my finger on it.

"Where are we going?"

"Go to the hotel and park at the back."

"Hell no, you took that bitch there which makes it no longer our spot. I'll go to the parking lot behind the truck stop."

"Where did you get this car from? This ain't the car you been driving."

"This is Brandi's new car."

I unzip my pants, pulling out my dick. "Get over her and take care of me since you want me to be your man."

She starts to roll her tongue around the head of my dick before she starts sucking it. I push her head down a little bit to make her mouth get a little moist. "Stop."

"Man just get up here," I say, pulling her up. She straddles my lap and lowers herself down onto my dick. Her grind is a little off, and I've had better but I nut, and I'm ready to go back to the office. I know that will tie her over for a little while.

I watch Lynn drive down the road until I can't see her anymore. I hop into the car and head over to the trucking company to see what Em is up to since she didn't answer the phone. I know it has something to do with this David guy, and I'm going to catch her in the act. She insisted on going to work to get work done when she could have stayed and worked from home, so I know there's more to it than what she's saying.

The building is full of movement in and out of the building. I don't know if it's because the business is growing or what. I'm about to find out though. After getting out of the car, I pass a couple of guys that could have been one of the sons of the man she sent to me to buy the property. One of them could have been David. Through the doors, I can see Em pushing herself around in the wheelchair to make her way around the office.

"Hey, lady, how is your day going?" I ask, walking in front of her so she can't continue on the path she was on.

"Yea, things are going good. Can you wait for me in my office? I have a video meeting to get to and I'll be right in, ok?" Her face is bright like she's really happy to be back at work.

I walk to her office and look at all the contracts she has scattered all over. She has been working her ass off just as much as I have at work. I sit in her chair and spot her journal. I usually wouldn't be bothered with reading what she's written but looking at the page, I see my name.

December 26th

I can't believe this has happened to me. I know it's not his fault, but if I would have gone to see the divorce attorney instead of him, I would have been fine. I wouldn't be sitting here contemplating cutting my leg off. The pain is getting to me. Markus has been on his best behavior the best I can see here lately, but I still don't trust him. It's hard to let him back in when every time he opens up his mouth, he says something that breaks my heart. He never encourages me anymore, he doesn't want to take me out anymore, he forgets my birthday, and our anniversary is tomorrow and I know he isn't going to remember. I guess I shouldn't either. I don't know why I still care. I don't know why I fight for the love of a man that couldn't give two fucks about me. Do I want to spend the rest of my life second to whomever he decides he wants to keep plunging his dick in and out of? I don't know. I just don't know. I'm just going to keep burying myself in my work and hope for the best.

Signed,

A broken hearted Ember

I can't believe this is how she is feeling even after we talked. I guess I can't expect her to change the way she feels overnight. I have to keep away from Lynn; as long as she's in the way it's going to make it harder to keep Em happy. I flip back a few pages until I see my name again.

November 19th

Today has been one of the worst days of my life. I know for a fact this man is cheating on me. I have seen the videos of him and the bitch he's fuckin' and I don't know if this shit is even worth it. Then, I talk to him about it and he makes it all be my fault because he decided to go fuck another woman. Make that shit make sense. Every single day he accuses me of cheating and being with other men when in reality it's him. He has been fuckin' this bitch for the last eight months, and he has paid for her to have an abortion and everything. He keeps lying to me as if I don't know. I know everything. His friends aren't exactly quiet about it and always slip up when I'm around. It's like they want me to know what type of nigga he is. I give him my all and then some. I give him my last and that's still not enough. The better question for me is when is it enough for me to finally want to let his cheating ass go? He will miss me when I'm gone and once I'm gone, there won't be no turning back for me. I will let the man that is going to love and cherish me be the man that I spend the rest of my life with. There was never supposed to be another after me. So since she came after we have spent so many years together, then maybe she's his soulmate and the one he is supposed to be married to instead of me. I'm tired of fighting a fight that I'm fighting by myself.

Signed,

A not-so-loved Em

I can't believe she feels this way about me. I can't believe she said all of this shit. What about the shit I go through on the daily basis? She only gives a damn about herself and what she is feeling. Maybe I shouldn't give a damn either since that's how she feels about all this shit. Everything I do is nothing to her. I mean nothing to her. I look up and see her in the doorway.

"Did you see something you like in my journal?" she asks mad as hell. "Why the fuck would you read my journal? That's your problem. You are always trying to control things and then use them against me. I don't know what kind of kick you get out of this shit, but it needs to stop!" she yells, wheeling herself over to the desk.

"I didn't know you felt this way about me. If I would have known that then I would have left you alone. It's like the only thing you think about is how you feel and fuck me, huh?"

"Right now. yes it's fuck you because that book is about my feelings and mine alone. If you were spending time talking to me instead of sinking your dick in every bitch that walks past you, then we wouldn't be having this conversation. You know what just get the fuck out!" she yells even louder, signaling Mya and Kacey to come running to her office.

The tears start to fall from her face and once again, I fuck up what little progress I've made now it's back to square one.

Lynn

This bitch is making it so hard to make this man understand we are supposed to be together. I mean, damn how hard is it for someone to leave a bitch alone? She's not all that and everything she can do, I can do and he won't have to worry about having someone talk back to him about it. His business wouldn't struggle at all. I will hold him down no matter what he wants to do. I just want my man to be my man and not have to worry about his on and off wife.

I have to find out what she has on him. I need to know what kind of hold she has that he can't let go of and will let her continue to call the shots. I scrape the phone from the table and walk around the kitchen. It is hard deciding to call this bitch or just let this shit run its course. I want to let it be, but this shit is moving too slowly.

"Fuck it." I dial so the number before talking myself out of it.

"Ok, I need these documents signed and returned within the week or we can't move forward, and Mya, can you please bring me a bottle of water to take this medicine?" I hear the song in her voice and it doesn't seem like there is anything wrong with her. He claims she is so hurt and she needs him to be there. This bitch can take care of herself.

"Who are you talking to on the phone?" a voice in the background asks.

"I don't know. Hello?" Her tone changes but still it hums like there is something she is happy about. Something she's looking forward to, and it pisses me off with every word. "I don't know what this is, but I will greatly appreciate it if you would stop playing on my phone." With a hint of anger, she ends the call.

"Who does this bitch think she is? This is getting out of hand; there can't be any more slip-ups. This shit ends now." I know the neighbors heard every word as I yelled it as loud as I could.

I have to get out of this house and clear my head because being here is making it harder to deal with this shit. "Hey, I need a ride somewhere if you aren't busy," I say, speaking with Tangy. I know she is always ready and down to ride when it comes to me getting my baby back. This man is supposed to be my husband and this is what I have to go through to get him to come home.

"Yea, where are we going?" she asks, but I hear the jingle of her keys in the background. That's my bitch right there. Always coming through for me.

"We are going to see where this nigga is since his whore of a wife seems to still be at work."

"What makes you think that woman is at work? Didn't he tell you she's hurt? I don't think a hurt woman is going to spend her time at work at least not a hurt woman with any kind of sense."

"Well, this bitch ain't got the sense God gave a billy goat because her ass is working and Markus is God knows where," I reply, wishing she could drive faster because there are a few places I need to hit to see if this man is coming home tonight.

"Well get your shit ready, and I'll be there in a few minutes."

This is going to be the longest few minutes of my life, but I know it's about to happen the way I see fit or he's gonna answer me tonight."

The dancing clouds across the skin with their orangish pink shade are so beautiful and make it all look worth it. Getting married under this kind of sky is what I would love to have for Markus and me.

"Ok, you never told me where we're going," Tangy says as we bend through a few corners.

"We need to pull up on Aaron. I know if he's not there, then Aaron knows where he is. And I don't have time to be wasting driving looking all over for him. I need him to finally give me some straight answers about this shit. I don't want to be left twisting in the wind. I'm not going to be his puppet that just goes along for the ride anymore," I explain. I hope she understands better now this is all not a game and it's time for Markus and me to be official and have our family.

"I'm glad you're ready to put your foot down with his ass."

"Just the man I need to see." I see Aaron walking to his truck at the edge of his yard. The car barely stops when I swing the door open. "Hey, old man!" I yell at him.

"I don't know who the hell you're calling old but anyway what do you want? If you are coming to look for Markus he's not here." He looks a little fed up.

"What's your problem? You've always had a stick in your ass. Do I need to arrange to have it removed?"

"Hell no, but you know you and Markus are going to get what's coming to you. That woman ain't crazy, and she is going to make you eat all that shit you talking."

"That bitch ain't got nothing on me and you just watch and see who has the last laugh." I am determined for him to see my point. He thinks this bitch is something he has no idea what she is in store for.

I slam the door and get back, and I'm even madder. "Hey, watch how you hold my baby," Tangy says.

I don't pay her any attention while scrolling through my call log, making sure to lock in on hubby. I tap my foot away as we make our way back through the town. "Where are you?" I ask, not giving him a chance to say anything.

"Well hi to you too, and what do you mean where am I?" Markus asks.

"I mean where the hell are you right now. I'm about to pull up."

"That doesn't matter right now." The voice of a woman follows him in the background, and my heart drops into my stomach.

"Don't tell me you are with this bitch right now," I call him on facetime. "I know you haven't been avoiding my calls because you are stuck under this bitch's ass."

"Look, I'm busy right now with my family. I'll call you when I have a chance."

"Answer the facetime, Markus," I call again. The beeping sounds as the whole call disconnects. "This nigga got me fucked up." I send another facetime call to his phone and his face appears on the screen. "What the fuck is your deal?"

"I know you don't understand this, but I have to make this shit work until Em is better. Your clingy ass needs to back off for a minute."

"How can you talk to me like that? I am technically the mother of your child. Just because you made me get an abortion doesn't mean shit."

"I know that. Do you think I don't know that? Look I love you, but I have to go handle this and stop calling like that. She is right here next to me, and she knows your fuckin' number so chill out."

The look in his eyes and the sincerity in his voice telling me he loves me makes all that anger and pain melt away. I know this man loves me, and he's going to do the right thing. I just have to wait and make the best of this, but Ember hasn't seen the last of me. Not by a long shot she hasn't.

"Let's stop at the liquor store and get something to drink. Since we don't have shit to do right now we might as well get fucked-up," Tangy suggested, pulling into the parking lot. This night is going to end on a good note, but I'm going to pay for it in the morning.

*****

The sun beams in through the window, hitting me directly in the face and sending a wave of pain through my whole body, and the drumming in my head seems to be getting louder. Opening my eyes makes me dizzy as hell as I try to make my way to the bathroom. I hear Tangy already letting go of everything she had to eat last night, so I continue through to the kitchen. I see pieces of the back door while I keep opening and closing one eye, trying not to let it stay open too long until I make it outside. The door is too far away but my sink is right there. I lean over the sink, flick on the garbage disposal, and throw up until there is nothing left but bile.

I thought that would make me feel better, but I couldn't have been more wrong. "Tangy, are you alright?"

"No. I'm dying," she says, slowly making her way into the kitchen. "Who the fuck got you on this Dusse? They need to be shot along with you because I have never had a hangover like this."

"Markus. This is the only shit he drinks, and I usually can handle this shit better but I don't know what happened last night. They must have given us an out of date bottle or something because that shit was hella strong."

"I'm about to call his limp dick ass right now."

"How do you know he has a limp dick?" I ask with a raised eyebrow.

"It's a figure of speech, jackass." She lifts her phone and blinks several times before she starts dialing numbers. It doesn't take long for him to answer. "Why the hell do you have Lynn drinking this bullshit?"

"Put it on speaker," I say, waving my hand in her face.

"This shit called Dusse. You know damn well we are not to be trusted with a bottle and our feelings."

"That has nothing to do with me. Y'all are two grown motherfuckas," Markus says just above a whisper.

"Anyway, what I need to know is if you are hiring right now. I need a job, and I know you pay well."

"No, you know my wife pays well," Markus corrects her, and I roll my eyes so hard I hear them pop.

"Well, are you hiring or not? I need a job."

"No, I'm not hiring right now. We have all the people we need and everybody has all the properties distributed between them," he explains.

"Ask him when is he going to come home."

"Did you hear her? Your woman wants you to come home," Tangy says closer to the phone. The line goes dead without an answer.

"That just started an argument." I laugh at the thought of Ember still under his ass listening to the whole conversation. That is how is going to learn one way or another.

Hanging around the house all day trying to recover from this hangover is not what I had planned. I should stick with Hennessy or something. The unexpected knock on the door brings back the headache I thought I could put behind me since it hadn't reared its thumping in a while.

"Open the door," Markus says from outside the door.

"I'm coming." I struggle to get up and let him in the house. "Where is your key?"

"I left it at home."

"You left my house key at your house? You know if your so-called wife comes up over her I'm going to shoot that bitch in her face, right?"

"You think that's what's going to happen? With the hatred she has built up for you, I don't think you would even see her coming."

"You are that confident in her taking me out, huh?"

"Please don't start."

"I'm going to let you two lovebirds have it," Tangy says, stumbling to the door.

"I'll walk you out." Grabbing her arm, I pull her close and walk out the door leaving Markus in the house. "I need another favor. I know you want to get home, but if you can make it back before Markus does, I need you to follow him so you can tell me where he lives."

"Why do you want to know where he lives?"

"Just in case. I need this man. Can you do it for me?"

"You know I got you. I have to go and take a nap in my cold house," she says, holding her head.

"Ok, I'll text you when he gets ready to leave," I say, putting her in the car.

Hurrying back to the house, I know this man is going to do me right. He better considering he has had me waiting on him for days now. Back in the house, I sit on his lap and pull him into a kiss.

"I've missed you."

"No, you don't because if you did you would do what I say and not what you want to do. When I tell you something it's for a reason. I don't care why you don't like my wife, but you're going to respect what I have going on or you won't be seeing any more of me." He looks angry and I must admit a little tired.

"I'm sorry, but you leave me here with nothing and you expect me to just be ok with the way you treat me. I'm your woman and I have feelings. I don't know how many times I have to tell you that shit." My eyes look into his, and it takes everything in me not to look away. There is something dark in his eyes, and it makes me scared and worried. "I want some dick." I unbutton his pants.

"No, not tonight."

"Why the fuck not? You must have fucked her and came over her with your dick dirty and shit."

"I don't know why you keep questioning me. I'm going to tell you some shit that I keep telling you. You knew what this shit was before we started. You knew I had a wife and you knew at the time I had no intentions of leaving her. So don't get this shit twisted. I let you know what it was from jump." He raises his voice at me. My heart starts to ache something serious, and I can't hold back the tears. How can he be this cold when he was the one that told me he was leaving her for me? He doesn't wait for me to get myself together before he's out the door.

I lay on the bed staring at the ceiling. I don't want this shit anymore. There has to be a better way to make this shit happen for me. It's time to get rid of this thorn in my side once and for all. He will be mine by any means necessary. I don't want to be the side chick. I want to be the main chick or the only one. I don't want to keep playing these games with him.

The phone rings. "Hello." Ember's voice comes on the line.

"How does it feel to know the man you love is in love with another woman?" I laugh as the line goes dead. She just doesn't know what kind of competition she has and hanging up is the worst thing she could have done. I let out another laugh, genuinely amused at the audacity of this woman.

My next call is the one I should have made a long time ago. "Brandi, I need a huge favor. May I please use your car for a couple of hours?"

"Yes, make sure you replace my gas," she says seriously. "Come grab the keys. I'll be in the shower."

I make my way around the block and grab the keys, making sure to lock her door behind me. I would have had Tangy take me again, but her ass is a little too nosy, and I need to get shit done without the second degree so I can concentrate.

I drive to the address Tangy gave me this morning, and I can see Markus isn't there. She should be making her way out of the house soon. It doesn't take long for her to walk out of the house wearing a big ass boot on her foot. This has to be some embarrassing shit to wear. I let out another laugh because shit keeps getting better and better.

Ember leaves the house and drives in my direction and it's now or never. I swerve into her lane, trying my damnedest to hit her, but the bitch hits the curb. I should go back and hit this bitch over the head with the crowbar in the trunk. I don't think Markus wouldn't take it too kindly if I killed his wife. At least not yet.

*****

I can't let this man keep doing me like this. He fucks me so good, I just forget all the stupid shit we have going on with this love triangle, leaving to me lay here looking around this room begging, craving, and needing him to touch me again. Then, I think about when he walks out the door he's going to be with his so-called wife. The one he claims he doesn't want to be with anymore. The same one he says he's just using to get what he needs out of the marriage and then he's going to be done with it. I don't think it's going to ever end or he's not going to ever get what he needs from the fuckin' marriage.

"Baby, I think we need to talk." I call Markus inside the bathroom.

"About what," he calls back, and I hear the irritation dripping from his words.

"I need you to be in here when I say this." The door opens and his face looks even worse than I thought. "I need you to take me seriously right now."

"I am being serious. I just don't want to ruin the night with any of the BS you always seem to find time to bring up when I'm around," Markus says, walking back to the bed.

"Ok, well this is going to be some of my BS because I need you to make a choice. Whatever choice you make I will understand, and I will let you be. You have to decide right now before you lay back down in my bed if you're going to be with me or your wife. Yes, I know what I signed up for, but you told me that you were going to leave her and you just wanted to secure whatever it is from her. I mean it's just getting old and it seems like you aren't going to get what you are supposed to be getting from her."

"If I have to make a choice right now it's going to be my wife. I have too much on the line for it to be left on the table. What I look like giving up everything we have worked hard for? She is going to find another man and he is going to be spending time where I'm supposed to be making our businesses work and reaping all the benefits of being with her. I'm not giving that up," Markus says, getting dressed.

"Where are you going?" I ask. "I know you aren't about to leave because I told you, you have to choose, are you?"

"Yes, I told you I didn't want to deal with this shit tonight and you had to start. I'm about to go get fucked-up, go home, and go to bed so I can work tomorrow." Without another word, he makes his way through the house and into the night. I don't know what I have to do to make that man see that I have everything he wants and needs; all he has to do is be here for it.

*****

I have been watching her for days, and she does the same thing day in and day out. I don't know how this bitch does it. I get tired from just watching her, and she still manages to make time to spend with Markus as long as he is around. I thought I could catch her slipping and fuckin' with another nigga, but she seems to be faithful at least for right now. I have to find something to use against her to make Markus want to leave. He has to want it or he's not going to do it. I can't believe he is holding on to this dream that she is his ticket to making money. Hell, I feel like if it hasn't happened in seven years then it's not going to happen.

I watch her step out of the house walking down the path to her car and this is it. The smile on my face is so big and mischievous that it hurts when I hear the sound of gunshots ring out one after the other. All four make my ears ring almost to the point I thought I was deaf. After opening my eyes I didn't even realize I had closed, I see Ember laying on the ground. Finally!

Ember

This is getting out of hand. I know being hit by a car may have been an accident but being shot at is something entirely different. The tires peel out as I lay on the ground as still as I can be. I look at the back of the car and it's the same car that ran me over before. I look around to see people coming out of their houses to look at what's going on.

"Ember, honey, are you alright?" Ms. Georgia asks and attempts to help me off the ground. Since we moved into the house, she has been a Godsend. She has made sure the house has been good when we take business trips and won't hesitate to call the police if something doesn't look right. She has talked me through a lot of things I have been through. When her husband died last year we, let her stay in the guest room until she was ready to go back home. She is the sweetest little old eight-five-year-old there is. I just hope I can live to see her age and have the wisdom she so soundly provides.

"Yes ma'am. I'm alright. I don't know who that was, but I think they are out to get me. If something happens to me you make sure to tell Markus about that car," I tell her, sounding almost like I was begging.

"I can do that and you know I have the video from the camera on my doorbell. We can show that to the police," she says.

"Yes, please can you save that for me and I will come by and get it later. God knows I needed a fresh cleanse because right at that moment, the sky opens up and the rain starts to fall on me heavily.

Running back into the house with this heavy ass boot, I dig through my purse for my phone. I have to call Mya and let her know I wouldn't be coming in. A text will be better, considering I don't want to deal with the third degree right now.

Me: Hey Mya, I'm having a bad morning. I'm not coming in today. If you need me for something feel free to call me, but everything should be smooth sailing for the day."

Mya: Ok. We will talk later and have a better day.

After lighting a few candles and putting on some soft music, I open up the windows and lay back on the bed. I have to get out of this. I don't know who or what is going on, but it's starting to get too dangerous. Lord, please if this has anything to do with Markus and his cheating ways please remove him from my life. I don't want to be caught up in any of his bullshit that's a result of him and the bullshit ass woman he's dealing with. Praying is the only thing I can do right now since trying to get Markus to see the error of his ways myself isn't working. I will remove my hands from him, and I won't beg him to stay no matter how much I love him and want to be with him. It hurts bad enough that he's cheating, but if something is going on and I have to pay for it because of his mistakes then I don't want it. I don't want to deal with that kind of hurt. The crazy part about it all is he doesn't have any remorse for the pain he has caused me and always finds a way to justify it to make it seem like he's never wrong.

I spend the rest of the day working on the new business plans and getting it going when the shit finally takes off. I see the shares and the likes going up right before my eyes. Then, the emails start to pour in about the event planning business that we have been wanting to start for so long. Opening the first request for a consultation, the butterflies in my stomach flutter around with so much excitement. I can't believe it finally happened. I don't know what I was afraid of, and I let fear hold me back from starting.

Picking up my phone, I scroll until I see Markus' name. I can't call him. No matter how much I want to I can't call him, and I can't let him in again. Besides, he wouldn't give a damn; if it's not his woman making it happen and making him happy, then he is going to find something wrong with it and complain. It hurts so badly knowing he doesn't care about me enough anymore to encourage me or want me to do better. I scroll back to the top of the list until Mya's number appears.

"Hey, are you busy?" I ask after she answers the phone.

"Not really at the moment. What's going on?" Mya ask. "I know it's something, you sound way too happy for it not to be."

"Well you know I was hesitating about starting the event planning service, right? Ok I did it, and I have fifteen consultation emails already and the website and social media pages are getting a lot of hits." I'm almost jumping in my bed with excitement.

"What? Are you serious? So you took the day off to work on something else?" she asks like she's caught me in something.

"No, I had a bad morning, but we aren't going to talk about that right now. I did it because I was sitting here doing nothing letting my thoughts get the best of me. I just had to do something to be a little productive."

"Wait, I forgot what you called it. I want to look at it."

"It's Blissful Events. The logo is purple and gold just like the one I had drawn up," I explain.

"Ok, I'm going to show everybody. I'll call you back but be ready to go to Illusions tonight to celebrate."

Illusions? I have to find something extra sexy to wear tonight. This is a celebration of something I have accomplished, and I'm not going to let my selfish husband stop me from having fun.

Pulling up to the club, I can already spot Mya and Shae in line waiting to get in. I hurry and make my way to them. "Hey, I finally made it."

"What did Markus say?" Mya asks, bracing herself for the fallout.

"I haven't seen Markus. He hasn't been home, and I'm not about to keep stressing myself out about what he's doing."

"Did you at least try to call him to tell him about the business?"

"No because lately, he has been doing a lot of complaining, and he doesn't treat me the same. So, I'm keeping it to myself until I get finished celebrating my little accomplishment."

"Of course, that's what we are about to do," Shae says, handing the bouncer outside the door some money as we walk past him.

"I think I've found our victims for the night." Mya nods to the end of the bar. "They are staring at the door like they're waiting on someone like us to walk through."

"I hope you're right. They might be waiting for somebody!" I yell in her ear over the music.

"Dressed like that," she gestures to my dress, "I don't think so. They are waiting for us, and if they were waiting for somebody else then they just missed out because they look happy to see us walking in their direction." She gives them a small wave.

I can't believe we just got in here, and she has already got her eyes on someone to pick up the tab. I guess no harm no foul, right? "And who are your friends?" one of the men asks smiling, looking between Shae and me.

"This is Em and Shae," she answers.

"Em, huh? I like that. May I buy you a drink, Em?" he says, pointing to the stool next to him.

"Yes, I'll have a martini, dirty." I look over to find out what Shae wants and she's gone to the dance floor with another guy. I can't do this. Mya seems to be having fun from the looks of it, but I can't in good faith do this. I look down at my phone and tap out a quick message.

Me: I can't do this. I can't entertain another man. I feel bad.

Mya: Lighten up. You aren't doing anything wrong. He's entertaining you and you are having a nice conversation. That's it.

"Let's dance!" Mya yells for us all to hear.

I follow her to the dance floor and let the music take me away from all my problems. "So what's your name?" I finally ask the guy I'm dancing with.

He smiles and leans into my ear. "My name is Jay. It's nice to meet a woman like you."

"What do you mean a woman like me? What kind of woman do you think I am?"

"From the looks of it, you are well-kept, but you bust your ass and go hard. I can tell the difference between you and your friends. They either don't have jobs or they work somewhere that doesn't pay them much."

"That's not true, they have good jobs. They're just frugal," I say.

"You look like you are the boss and everybody answers to you. You even look like you may be an asshole boss, but you make sure you get your money."

"You can tell all that just by looking at me?"

Jay laughs again but this time, I can tell he's hiding something. "No, I drive for one of the companies you do trips for. I recognized you the moment you stepped through the door."

"Oh, so you're gonna play me like that. I see how you do."

We continue to dance the night away while I watch what I have to drink so I can make it home. Hanging out with Jay for the night wasn't so bad, and I guess Mya was right. It's not doing anything wrong. I guess it's time for me to have a little fun too.

*****

Staring at the business card I keep flipping through my fingers, I keep contemplating doing business with this man. He has tried to do business with us before, but his vibe is off, and considering he told her he wanted to take me to breakfast I don't want to give him the wrong idea. This shit is going to be strictly business. I just don't have time to be dealing with Kenneth Dolton right now.

"Dolton, doing business with you would put us both in a position to make a lot of money and it will be less work for you and your drivers," I say, sitting across from him at Lula's Lux. This restaurant usually takes a restaurant at least five months before you get a free table, but with Kenneth Dolton anything is possible. The infamous Mr. KD has everyone eating out of the palm of his hand, even the elites are waiting in line to have a sit-down with him.

"You're right this could make us both money, but what I want to know is, are you ready to get a divorce and be in the arm of a man that can take care of you?" His eye narrows seductively as he speaks, and if I

could honestly say if my husband wasn't giving him a run for his money in the sexy department, then I may have had to take him up on this offer.

"Look you know I'm not leaving my husband, and if that's the only reason you invited me to this meeting, then I can cut this short," I say, looking at his peanut butter brown skin warm and smooth, framing his sexy juicy ass lips. His goatee is solid black with a few lines of gray in it and his sparkling dark brown eyes seem to light up every time he mentions me leaving Markus.

"No, that's not the only reason, but it's a reason. I know you love that man, hell I don't think I would understand you sticking around if you didn't. But to be honest, don't you think you deserve better?"

"I know what I deserve, and he is what I deserve. We are building our empire together from nothing so once we make it, then we will both appreciate it even more while growing our bond as a couple."

The glare on his face shifted as if he wants to say something, but he kept quiet. "You know I can respect that, but let's have dinner and we can talk shop another time. We should enjoy the evening."

This man is going to drive me up the wall with his mixed signals. I can't wait until he signs this contract, and I won't have to deal with him directly anymore.

The memory floods back and sends my body into chills after thinking about the way he made me feel. I don't know if I can deal with that right now, considering what I'm going through with Markus. He might be the answer to everything I need.

I won't waste another minute before sending the text and talking myself out of it again.

Me: Hey Mya, go ahead and set up the meeting with Dolton. Make sure you make the reservations somewhere nice, but not breaking the bank. He's not calling the shots this time.

Mya: Thank you. It's about time.

Me: No ma'am it's not that kind of party. We just need this man's business to increase our contacts. Don't get it twisted. I should let you go and maybe he will make you leave Lance.

Mya: Alright, alright I'm cool. I'll set it up for you.

I don't know why she is so keen on wanting me to leave my husband. I know her past was bad, but I have to see this through on my own without being persuaded.

Another message comes through on my phone.

Mya: He wants to take you to breakfast.

I look over at the empty spot where my husband is supposed to be, and I can't help but feel a little ping of regret in the pit of my stomach. Maybe this is a good time for me to go ahead and step away from the life I built with Markus and look into dating again. Why should I sit around and wait for our divorce when he's already gotten a head start? I watch the night sky out my window until I feel the sweep of my dream pulling me in.

Warmth and the glow of the morning sun wake me to the chiming of the doorbell being rang repeatedly. The clock on my nightstand shows it at eight thirty, but I don't know who or why someone would be at my door this time of the morning. I race downstairs, attempting to put my robe on. My heart starts to flutter a little faster out of confusion, fear, and anxiety.

"Who is it?" I yell around the corner, still trying to tie the belt of the robe.

"It's me," Markus says. "Open the door, Em."

"What do you want, Markus? I don't think you should be here," I call through the door again. He is not going to make this divorce an easy one. We have everything already separated and papers filed. I just need the judge to sign and make it official. Hopefully, then he will leave me alone.

"I need to talk to you for just a second. I promise it won't take long. Five minutes." The pain in his voice starts to sound like misery and almost sobs.

Opening the door, I see his eyes are red with bags under them like he hasn't slept in days. Running my hand over my belly, his eyes drift down my body until it stops where my hand rests on top of my baby bump.

"Markus, I don't want to do this right now."

"Em, is....is that my baby?" He points to my belly. "Tell me that's my baby." He closes his eyes as if praying to Allah for our baby to be his.

"Markus, we shouldn't get into this right now. Will you please just go?" I push the door shut and watch his eyes beg me to stop. Tears start to roll down my face, but I can't let him see he has gotten to me. I need him to leave now.

"Em, please open the door and tell me if this is my baby."

"Yes, Markus he is your baby," I whisper through the door.

"What? Say it again, Em."

"Yes," I let out loudly. "Yes, he's yours."

"Talk to me, Em. I want to be there for you and our son. Please put a stop to this divorce. I want my family. I love you."

"Markus, I can't do this right now please just leave."

"Why won't you talk to me? What's so hard about talking to me for five fuckin' minutes?"

"I don't want to talk to you because I don't want to get sucked into your web right now. I have plans and if I let you get to me, then I won't go through with them."

"What plans, Em? What are you planning on doing?"

Frustrated, I swing the door open so hard the gust of air fans the bottom of my robe open. "I am planning on moving at the end of the month to a new state to have a fresh start. So you don't have to worry about the baby."

"What the fuck are you talking about? You just told me you're having my baby and now you're telling me you're moving with my son to another state. You got me fucked-up if you think I'm gonna let that happen."

"You don't have a choice." A pain shoots through my lower abdomen, and I hunch over trying to breathe until it passes.

"What's wrong? Is something wrong with the baby?" Markus

grabs me, wrapping me in his arms. I miss feeling his touch and being wrapped in his embrace. I love the way this man covers me with his strength.

He walks me back upstairs to the bed. I lay down and try to stretch out to help the pain go away. "Thank you, but you can go now," I say, wincing with the pain.

"No, I'm not leaving until I know you're alright." He lays next to me and wraps his arms around me rubbing my belly. The baby starts to kick against his hand. "Look, you see he knows his daddy is home."

"Daddy is not home. Daddy is about to go back home," I correct him. I get lost in his touch and drift off to sleep. Why does loving this man comes with so much pain?

The alarm clock blares, waking me and I run my hand across my flat stomach wishing the dream was real. I wish I would have a piece of the man I love to have forever. I push the button to stop the blaring before I get a headache from the noise. I feel the bed shift under me. and I look over to see Markus laying in bed next to me.

I don't waste any time getting dressed because talking to him about anything is not on the agenda this morning, and I don't want to be late. I slip into my strapless form fitting beige dress and pull my white blazer over it. I check myself in the mirror, and Markus is laying in the bed looking at me.

"You weren't going to tell me you're leaving?" he asks, not moving a muscle. "Come here. I've missed you."

"You wouldn't have to miss me if you brought your ass home every night," I say just above my whisper.

"What?"

"No, I have to get to work. I don't have time to go back and forth with you." My phone rings on the nightstand. I walk over to pick it up when Markus quickly grabs it and answers it.

"Hello." He looks at the phone and then at me. "So who do you have calling your phone? I know it was another man because his coward ass hung up."

"I don't have anyone calling me and they just don't want to talk to you. This is my business phone and no one is used to you answering the phone," I try to explain.

"This the nigga I have seen you with isn't it?"

I let out a deep laugh at his stupidity. "You are the only one being unfaithful. Don't try to put your bullshit on me with your blame-shifting, narcissistic ass." I grab my things and walk out of the bedroom and then clean out the house without my coffee or anything. I just need to get away from this man as quickly as possible.

I look at the clock and see I'm late meeting with KD. I have to brace myself for what's to come. I don't want to let him slip away this time, and I am determined to seal the deal. No matter the cost.

Markus

This is not the way things are supposed to be. I can't lose Em like this and to another man. She is supposed to be my forever, and I'm letting her slip right through my fingers. I love her, and I have to find a way to get her back. I have never seen her as confident as she is now, and she knows it. She can feel it and it shows when she walks and talks now. The bumps on the ceiling help me form a plan to get me back because I know she can give two fucks about me right now. She has the attention of someone else, and she is falling for him. I can see that shit in her eyes.

The sting on my arms feels like fire. "Do you hear me talking to you, Markus Ballard?" She tilts her head to the side.

"No, I didn't, and don't hit me anymore."

"When are you going to bring the rest of your clothes?"

"I don't know and what do you mean the rest of my clothes?"

"You have clothes right there and some in the dresser."

"I've been looking for my damn clothes. Em knows when my shit goes missing. She asks me about that shit, and I don't even remember bringing that shit over."

"You wore it here and when you take a shower, you just change and leave it here. I can't believe you're still playing house with that bitch. You need to get that shit straight and come home."

"I'm not about to do this with you." I get up and pull my boxers and pants on. "I think it's time we take a break. I need to focus on Ember before she takes everything and leaves me with nothing."

"Look, I don't know what kind of bullshit games you're playing, but it's not going to work over here. This is the last time I'm going to say it. If you can't get your shit together then you need to stay your bum ass over there with the bitch that can't give you kids and that doesn't do anything for you." She blows up.

"I have to go." I grab my things and walk out of the house.

I drive through town just letting the city pass me with no particular destination. I just ride, ignoring all the phone calls coming in. Aaron, Lynn, Ember, and Julian call but I can't bring myself to talk to anyone just yet. I finally run up to a liquor store; Dusse is the only thing that's going to get me over the hump. Drunk Tuesday it is.

*****

The tapping on the window starts to get on my nerves. "What? What do you want?" I yell at the blurry figure standing outside my car door.

"Sir, you can't park here." The figure of a man standing there starts to clear up little by little.

"I'm sorry. I'm moving." I wipe my eyes and look around the car. Everything seems to be in order, so I push start the car and pull out of the parking lot. The ride home goes by quickly, and I find myself sitting outside my house looking at my beautiful wife through the window walking around doing God knows what.

As I watch her, I feel the love she has for me and what I have for her ready to burst out of my chest. This is the woman I am supposed to be with and yet, I still fuck up. I make her all these promises and break them like they are twigs beneath my feet. I can't even provide a legit reason for this shit. All this time, and I still fuck up for no reason. She gathers her things and walks out the door talking on the phone.

"No, I'll be right there. I have to stop and get the platter and we can have the meeting. I need this event to go off without any problems," Ember says, getting inside the car.

She drives away without a single clue of me sitting out here watching her. More often than not when she leaves the house, I watch her and sometimes follow her. I pray I don't ever catch her going to another man's house. I don't think I will be able to let them live if she goes to see another man. I love her so much, I can't stand to see her with another man. I can't stand knowing that another man is getting what is supposed to be for me.

I make the night special by making dinner for Em and setting the table for our candlelight dinner. I see the lights flash against the window, and I place the baking dish of mac and cheese on the table. I wait for her to walk through the door, and I meet her with a single lily in my hand for her.

"Good evening, sexy lady," I say, handing her the flower. "I have a night to remember planned for you." I hold out my hand to her. I can tell she doesn't want to, but I take a step forward. "Baby, please let me do this for you."

She takes my hand. "What's this all about, Markus?"

I lead her to the kitchen and pull out her chair for her. "This is your night, and I want to make it special for you."

"I can see you went through a lot of trouble. So how are you going to make this night special?" I see a hint of a smile on her face.

"You'll just have to see."

"Markus, I don't want to play games with you." She stands and walks out of the kitchen. She starts to take off her clothes as she ascends the stairs.

"Em, please come back." I run up the stairs to catch her before she is completely naked although I would prefer it that way.

"No, Markus, I don't want to keep investing myself in a man and a relationship that's not going to change. I want to be loved unconditionally. I want to be happy and spend the rest of my life not worrying if the man that's supposed to be loving me is out loving on someone else. I can't get that with you."

"Baby, I will change. I don't want to lose you. I need you."

"You say all that constantly and you still manage to go back on your word."

"Ember you know me. I don't know how I can make this right. I just need to get this out of my system, but I'm done."

"Markus, you always say and do this. I can't trust you anymore. I don't feel safe with you."

I can see the pain and fear in her eyes, and she is serious about it all. I don't think I'm going to be able to change her mind. I've lost the love of my life.

*****

I have to do something to get my baby back. Walking into the building, everyone is busy as usual so I know it's going to be the same with her. She is gifted at making this business work and getting these drivers what they need for their loads. I walk into her office and see her on the phone tapping away on her computer. I watch her in amazement and realize she built this from nothing into a major dispatching of a freight company. She did all of this on her own and she is still doing it. Most CEOs are hands-off and let the workers handle it, but she is right here with everyone else making sure everything is running smoothly. It makes me love her that much more to know she is working her ass off for this.

She finally looks up at me and holds a finger in the air, putting me on pause. I smile at her and take a seat across from her. She lays the phone down and throws her head back against the back of the chair. "Hey, I am really busy and I can't handle anything right now," she says with a little defeat swirled in with her words.

"Well let me take you away for a while. I mean that's why you have people working for you so you can take a break," I plead my case.

"I have too many drivers to handle today. Today is the start of their new trips and I have them all planned out but getting them on the phone and in the truck is proving to be difficult right now."

"You said you were going to let what's her face have more responsibility. So let her do it and have Mya oversee her to make sure it's done right." The wheels turn in her head, and also see she needs a little time to herself to breathe.

"Fine, where are we going?"

"Wherever you want to go." I grab her hand and lead her out of her office. I watch her walk into Mya's office for a brief moment before returning to me in the hall. Mya glares at me as if she doesn't approve of our little outing, but I don't care because this is for my baby.

I take her to the car, and I see her whole body relax in the seat. The sunset of the evening covers the sky, making her even more beautiful as we take a drive through the city. I miss the times we used to spend like this. I just have to get it all back and not let it go this time.

"You want to make a quick stop at your favorite smoothie shop?" I ask.

"Yes, please get me the strawberry cream passion fruit smoothie. Make it a large, please."

"Anything for you, my love." Pulling into the drive thru, it's busier than usual and the parking lot is like a club with all the people standing around.

"Hey, handsome." A woman walks by waving with her ass twisting a little harder than needed to try and get my attention. Ember looks over at me and the vibe of the car shifts.

"What, babe?" I ask, watching the darkness fill her eyes.

"Nothing. It's all good."

"Yes, it is. I didn't do that."

"It's cool. I just want to go home."

"You want to go home now? We were having fun."

"Yes we were, but not anymore. I just want to go home."

The drive home was awkward and full of tension and silence. Pulling into the driveway, I know it's going to get worse from here. Without a word, Ember gets out of the car and leaves me sitting there. I don't know if I should get out or not. I don't want to keep digging myself into a hole that I can't get out of. Pulling my face down under my hand, I dread her walking into the house without me. I take a look at her just before shifting into reverse, and she's standing there looking at me. Waiting. I return the car to park and get out to join her at the door.

"Are you alright?" I ask, wondering what she was waiting for.

"Yes, aren't you going to come in?" she asks, and the look of desire for me is one filled with sincerity and love. I know this woman loves me, but I hope I don't mess up whatever this is.

"If that's what you want then yes. I want to come home," I say maybe pushing the envelope a little bit.

"Well, come on." She steps into the house. She doesn't stop to look back but continues up the stairs. Following her, I can't help but get excited about being at home and in my bed with my baby.

I stand at the door watching her take off her clothes and all her curves are just as beautiful as ever. Her ass is round and plump, the breasts big and calling out to me, and not to mention the fullness of her lips opening up to a sexy smile that I've missed waking up to every morning. It's something about being connected to this woman that makes it hard to live without her. I can be myself and have no worries about being judged.

She's naked and walks over to the bed. "Are you going to stand that all night or are you going to get in the bed?" she asks.

"I was just watching and admiring the beautiful work of art that stands before me."

"Oh you have jokes tonight, I see." She lets the shyness wash over her face.

I shed the layers of clothes I have on to join her.

The covers are just as soft as I remember. "Damn I miss this bed." I put my arms around her. "I love you."

"I love you too." Her light brown eyes look up at me. "Listen I don't know where we go from here, but if we are going to make this work then you have to do a lot better. I know I'm not blameless, but your unfaithfulness is what got us here. I will do my best to make the changes needed for us to be better too," she says. Tears fills her eyes.

"Does that mean I can come home now?" I ask, nuzzling my nose into the neck.

"Yes, you can come home." Pulling her into a kiss, I can't help getting aroused instantly. Damn this woman knows how to drive me crazy. Her hand strokes my length, and I try my hardest not to let out a moan.

I can't wait. I pull her down in the bed, settling between her legs. Looking down at her, she's ready and the heat comes from her pussy. She's so wet it makes me feel like I've been thirsting for her. I push inside of her and watch her eye roll to the back of her head. Her moans are like music and with each thrust, she lets go more and more. She grips my back, pulling me to her, and I sink deep inside her. The moans filled with pleasure and a hint of pain follow. I kiss her lips to muffle the sound coming from her, and I increase the pace threatening to nut inside her the faster I go, but I can't help it. Her pussy's so damn good, I don't want to stop. I stop and pull out.

"No, no, no baby don't stop. What are you doing?" she begs.

"I'm not ready to end it yet."

"Come on, baby. Make love to me."

Making love to the love of my life gives me life. I can't stand someone else thinking they can take my blessing. This is for me and no one else, and I will do whatever to make sure she stays.

"Turn around and put your ass in the air," I tell her, looking at her ass bounce as she gets on all fours. I slap her ass. "You gonna throw that ass back for me?"

Her arch is deep as I slide inside her, and I realized I've fucked up. She starts to rock on my dick hard and her ass bounces nicely, making it harder to hold this shit together.

"Baby you're gonna make me nut," I tell her.

"I know." She goes harder and the clap of our bodies echoes in through the room. I grip her hips and force myself inside her hard repeatedly as the nut shoots out of my dick. Her moans grow louder with each one, and her juices mix and spill out of her pussy as I continue to thrust. "I didn't know you missed me so much." She laughed, laying down. "You get the wet spot." Looking at the bed, I realize she had squirt all over both the bed and me.

I don't even have the strength to put up a fight. I put the comforter down, lay down, and let the sex coma take over. It feels good to be home.

*****

I woke up to the most amazing head I've gotten in a long time from my baby. I still can't find why in the hell I want to fuck off on his woman. I have yet to find anyone that is like her, but there is something about being outside that makes it hard to stay faithful. I know she's worth more than anything I can give, but I can't.

The phone rings on the car radio as I pull into the gas station. "We have someone in the office that's looking for the Cove property. They are willing to pay above market value for the house. How soon can you get here?" Julian asks, whispering into the phone.

This property has been a pain in my ass and finding someone that wants it is taken a lot of stress off of me. "I just stopped for gas, and I'll be there in about fifteen minutes." I hurry inside the gas station to pay. "Good morning. May I get thirty on pump seven, please?"

"Good morning to you too. You can have anything you want." The woman standing behind the counter stares at me. She looks older, but she can handle her own. "Where are you off to this morning?" she asks, batting her eyes at me in a flirtatious way.

"Work." I laugh.

She slides me the receipt, and I look down at the number written on it. "Call me, and I can help you have a better morning. "

I look at the number and back at her. Her dark brown eyes are still fixed on me with her small frame. She's not much to look at but her lips damn sure look like she has some fire ass head. "Alright. Thank you." I take the number and shove it into my pocket before exiting the store.

I can't believe I did that shit. Pulling the number from my pocket, I should throw this shit away. The gas handle clicks. Shaking my head, I put it back in my pocket. I have more pressing things to think about right now than to wonder about this damn number. Fuck, why is this shit so hard? This has to be a fuckin' addiction.

Ember

This weekend is going to be one for the books. I know I shouldn't put all my eggs in one basket with this man of mine, but I have to put in some effort to make this work. I can't be half-ass if I want him to give me everything. I sit here scrolling through the pictures of the treehouse, and I'm excited to spend this time with my husband to try to get us back on the right path.

My office door opens. "Did you get the Airbnb booked?" Kacey asks.

"Yes, come look at the way it's going to look when we get there. I think this is going to be something that makes him realize what we have is worth it." I show her the picture of the treehouse. "I have to call the host when we are about twenty minutes away so she can have all the candles lit."

"That looks amazing. Have you shown Mya and Shae yet?"

"No, I haven't because I don't think Mya is going to agree with what I'm doing." The soft knock on the door ends the conversation. "Come in," I call through the tall figure on the other side of the door. I'm starting to regret getting my office door frosted.

"Hi, Mrs. Ballard." Mr. Morton walks through the door. "I was stopping in to touch bases with you since I haven't heard anything from you."

"Kacey, will you give us a few minutes?" I wait until the door is closed and the silhouette has disappeared from outside the door. "Yes sir, I have been really busy, and I have taken your words to heart. I want to make sure this is what I need to do before I do it. I don't want to waste your time or mine so before I walk away, I want to make sure I have done all I can as a wife for our marriage."

"I can't say that I'm angry, but I was looking forward to you being a free woman one day." He laughed. "I wish you all the best and you have my number. I will be here if you need me." He starts toward the door.

"Yes sir, thank you again for all your help." I let out the air in my chest of relief. I know I have closed a door that needed to be closed at least for now. I have to be all in. I can't keep one foot out the door. I have to make this work for the sake of our family.

I gather my things inside the cart and make sure all the luggage is properly packed and ready to go. While driving to Markus' office, I get all giddy inside just thinking about the look on his face when he sees where we are going. I climb in the car and call Markus. It rings and dread finds me with every ring.

"Hello," he finally answers the line. "Babe, can you hear me?"

"Yes, can you leave? I have a surprise for you."

"Yes, what's going on?"

"Well, I'm bring you a change of clothes because you're gonna have to be comfortable for the trip," I say, trying to contain my excitement.

"Where are we going, baby?" Markus asks with confusion in his voice.

"I can't tell you or it wouldn't be a surprise. Just know it's going to take a little time so you can take a nap and get well rested," I explain, getting ready to pull into his parking lot. "I'm getting ready to pull in. Come grab your gym bag so you can change."

"I can change in the car. I'm walking out right now." He hangs up the phone, and I can't wait to see what the weekend holds for us.

I pull into the rest stop to go to the restroom. "I'll be back, baby."

"Wait for me. I need to go to the bathroom too."

We make our way up the path to the restroom, and just as I close the door a hand stops it from closing. "Wait. Let me come in with you," Markus says.

After using the restroom, we make our way out to wash up. His hands turn me to face him and his mouth covers mine, deepening the kiss as our tongues dance with one another. Lifting me in the air, he sits me on the sink and pulls my shorts to the side. I pull down his basketball shorts, exposing his hard length ready to make his way inside me. The cold mirror behind me and his body pushes against me as his dick enter my pussy, making me wetter with every single touch. Shifting on the sink, he plunges inside me. My juices spill over and his thrust goes deeper. The ecstasy pours through my veins.

"Baby, I'm about to cum," I sputter out, and his force gets harder and faster, bringing me to release all over his dick.

"This dick is good, baby."

"Yes." I pant as his grunt quietly slips out. I feel his nut inside me. "Damn, baby, this was a good idea to stop for this pick me up."

"Pick me up? We're gonna see how long this pick me up lasts," I joke with him. We wash up properly and make our way back to the car to get on the road.

The drive is uneventful after the rest stop as Markus sleeps. With excitement building back inside me, I call the host. "Hello Mrs. Johnson, I am about twenty minutes out, and I just wanted to give you the heads-up to go ahead with the candles.'

"Yes, Mrs. Ballard. I will have that taken care of right away. Be safe."

Just as she says that, the rain starts to drizzle from the sky. I let out a soft sigh, "Thank you."

The light from the treehouse lights up windows and it looks like the treehouse is a cabin in the sky. I nudge Markus. "Baby, get up. We made it." I smile at him as he rubs his eyes and adjusts to the seat.

"Where have we made it to?" he asks, still rubbing the sleep out.

"Look." I point to the treehouse.

"Damn, is that where we're staying?" he asks, amazed at the sight.

"Yes, this is ours for the weekend. Now, come on. I need to show you what's inside." I open the door and the soft sprinkle of the cold rain trickles my skin. The feeling is breathtaking. "Help me grab the bags, please."

"Bags? Baby, what have you done?" Markus asks, walking around to meet me at the trunk.

"I packed our stuff for the weekend. Now, come on."

We quickly grab the bags and walk across the rope bridge to the treehouse. Stepping inside, the candles dance in the dark room. We walk around the house and see the living room covered in candles. The kitchen is laid with a spread of fruit with chocolate and a full three course meal on the kitchen table. Inside the bedroom, the view of the trees and the sky full of stars light up the night sky and the rain covering the windows. In the tub, that bath is drawn, the jets are going, and the bubbles set the mood.

"Ok, baby I see you. I love it, but what's the occasion?" Markus asks, still walking around and taking in the rest of the house.

"I just wanted a weekend with my husband without either one of us having to worry about work and enjoying one another." I enclose my arms around his neck. "I love you, and I need us to get back to where we once were."

"This is a good start." He pulls me into a kiss. "Where should we start?"

"How about the bathroom?"

I can't wait to ride the waves of his dick while enjoying the massage of the jets. It's the most relaxing thing we can do and much needed.

*****

The sunrise climbing over the horizon is the most beautiful view I have ever seen. I roll over and look at Markus still sleeping. This weekend has been what we have needed for a long time. I get up and run a bath to get our morning started for the last day being away from the outside world. The pregnancy test sitting on top of my bag tempts me to take the test sooner than I'm supposed to. I'm only four days late, but these last few days. I pushed the idea of being pregnant out of my mind but when looking at the test I have a war of words with myself on if I should get it out the way or not. I hear him moving in the bed and take the test from the bag. I finish, lay the test on the sink, and wait as I add the bubbles and start the jets on the tub. These two minutes seem to be more like twenty, but when I turn it over, *pregnant* appears on the indicator. Heart racing, I cover my mouth to muffle my screams of happiness. I can't believe I'm finally going to have a baby. I'm going to have my husband's baby.

I get into the tub, making sure it's not too hot considering my news and let the bubbles relax me while I wait for Markus to wake up. I replay everything we have been through in my head like a movie, and I don't know if he's going to be truly happy with the baby. I weep at the thought of not having my husband there to raise our baby together. I can't do this to our child, and I refuse to let someone else do it.

"Good morning, beautiful." Markus walks into the restroom, planting a kiss on top of my head.

"Good morning." I wipe my face before turning to face him. "What would make your day?" I ask.

"Baby, you have done everything to make my year. I don't need anything else," he says, washing his hands after using the restroom. "You want some company?"

"Yes, I would love some." He climbs in and I straddle his lap as he sits down. "I have something to tell you, and I don't want you to freak out." I look into his eyes and wait for him to respond.

He looks at me with a raised eyebrow. "Are you going to tell me?"

"I'm……um….." I shuffle my words. "I'm pregnant." I close my eyes.

"You're what?" he asks as his smile lights up his whole face. "Tell me this is for real."

"Yes, the test is over on the sink. I just took it before I got in."

"We're gonna have a baby?" He lifts me and kisses my stomach. "I'm your daddy, little man."

"Little man?" I ask. "How do you know it's going to be a he?" He sits me back down on his lap.

"I just know." He kiss me so passionately. I can't believe this is what it took for him to finally give in to me.

The morning starts with my husband making love to me and making me feel like the only woman in his world. That's all I've ever want and all I will ever need.

*****

The weekend was wonderful, and I was the center of his world. I just need him to keep the same energy now that we've returned home. The office phone rings. "Hello." I speak into the phone.

"I just wanted to see if you were back. I'm running a little late," Mya answers.

"Yes, I'm here."

"Ok, I'll be there in like two minutes."

Kacey walks in the door without knocking. "Hey, Ember, you're in early and it looks like you're glowing. I take it things went well this weekend?"

"Yes, things went well." I smile. "But I'm not telling you anything until Mya gets here because I am not going to repeat myself. You are going to have to wait. She should be walking through the door any minute."

Just then, the door opens and an out of breath Mya walks through the door. "Tell us everything," she says, bending over to catch her breath.

"Damn, did you run in here?" Kacey asks.

"Yes. Now spill all the tea."

"Ok, first I want to tell you both not to freak out. I'm not about to be picking either one of you off the floor." I look from one to the other of them and watch them give each other a look. "I'm pregnant." I let go of the breath I was holding.

"What the hell? Are you sure?" Mya asks, looking at Kacey.

The look on Kacey's face gives me a bad vibe, and Mya doesn't seem happy with my news. "What's wrong?" I ask, looking at both of them. I know they're hiding something from me.

"I have something to tell you, and I don't want you to get too upset, but I need you to know," Kacey says, taking a long deep breath.

"Ok well spit it out," I urge.

"A friend of mine is sleeping with Markus." The room goes silent, and I try to wrap my head around what she just told me.

"What do you mean? How do you know this?"

"I have the pictures and the video that she took of them. I didn't want to believe it when I saw it, but it's him," Kacey says, handing me her phone.

I flip through the pictures until I reach the video. My eyes start to burn as I watch my husband fuck another woman. I see his face clearly, and he looks just like he does when he's making love to me. My soul is hurting and crying out for help, and there is no one I can call out to. I clear my throat and hand the phone back to Kacey.

"Are you alright?" Mya asks, letting the tears well up in her eyes.

"Yes, I'm fine." I clear my throat again. "I'll take care of this. Thank you for bringing this to my attention."

I look at Mya, and she springs into action. "Let's go and give her a minute." She ushers Kacey out. "I think we should have waited to tell her. She was so happy and now she's probably gonna have an abortion and fall off the face of the earth."

"I didn't mean to ruin it for her, but I thought she should know instead of trying to make something with someone that's not going to take her and their relationship seriously," Kacey explains herself.

I can't let this stop me from having the family I have wanted with my husband. This was before we had our weekend together and made it official that we are going to do everything possible to make sure we are true to one another. I can't do this without him, and I refuse to. I have to get to the bottom of it

I walk into Markus' office as if nothing is wrong. I can't let anyone see I'm upset. We are the united front and keeping people out of our business is the number one priority from this moment forward. I will not be the laughingstock of this anymore and respect is something they will have for our marriage or pay the price for not doing so.

I can see down the hall his office lights are off and he's not in, so I return to the receptionist. "How long has Markus been out of the office?"

"He left about ten minutes ago. He and Julian are out closing the deal on the Cove property," she explains.

"Ok thank you." I walk back out on the street when I get shoved against the wall.

"Don't scream or I will kill you. Nod if you understand." I nod as instructed by the man standing behind me. "Now I am going to tell you this once and only once, or I will come back and gut you like a fish." The blade of the knife scraps against my back.

"What do you want? You can have all the money in my purse just please leave me alone. I'm pregnant," I plead with him.

"This nigga Markus you can't seem to get enough of, you are going to leave him alone. He has a family and it doesn't include you. His wife is stressed as hell and needs her husband to be focused on her. She has lost a child behind being stressed with the fact he can't get enough of you. If I have to come back, I am going to fuck you then kill you and hang you out for the world to see. Do I make myself clear?"

I nod my head confused. "Who is his wife? I didn't know he was married."

"My sister. Now leave him alone." The man scraps the knife against my back, firmly drawing blood.

"Hey, get the fuck off her!" a voice yells, getting closer. I look to see Markus and Julian running over to help me. The guy drops the knife and runs off. "Baby, are you alright?" Markus asks, pulling me into a hug.

"I'm fine. He told me your wife doesn't want you to be with me anymore and if he has to come back, he's going to kill me." The tears flood my face.

"What the fuck he mean my wife? Baby, please don't listen to him. I promise you are my only wife. I don't know what the fuck he's talking about. You have to believe me."

"I don't care anymore. I'm going home." I walk away, get into the car, and leave. The tone of Markus' voice echoes behind me, but I don't stop or look back at him.

I have to get away. I walk into the house and fall to my knees, letting the pain engulf me. I let it all out. I don't hold anything back. After laying there for a few minutes, I pick myself up and go to my bedroom. Climbing the stairs takes a lot out of me, and I try my damnedest not to give in. I finally make it to the bed and take off my clothes. This can't be happening to me. It's not just my life anymore it's about my baby, our baby, and I'm not going to have it taken by someone that he has a history with.

Markus comes into the house calling my name until he reaches our bedroom. I don't give him a chance to say anything else. "Who is she and where does she live?" I ask.

"What?"

"Who is she and where does she live? You better not lie to me or I'm going to come down on you and hard." I never turn away from the window to look at him.

With a deep sigh, he says, "She lives at 1572 Hannah Ave. What are you about to do?"

"I'm about to take care of the shit you can't seem to get under control. You can't seem to keep them in line, so I'm going to take it."

"No, babe, you're pregnant. I will take care of it."

"You won't be taking care of anything, and if I hear or see you going there it's going to be a problem." I stand and walk into the restroom.

*****

"I need you to get Kacey and Shae together and meet me at Coffee and Cakes."

"What's wrong?" Mya asks.

"I just need to meet with you all, and I will fill you in on everything. Meet me there in about fifteen minutes. Don't be late."

I sit at the back of the shop and wait for them all to walk in. This has to be done with finesse and accuracy, and I need them to know what they are about to get into. They all enter together, talking among one another before they reach the table.

"I hope some shit is about to pop off because I'm ready to take some shit down." Shae bounced up and down, pounding her fist into her palm.

"Sit down and we can get started. Now before I tell you anything, I need for you all to know we can't fuck up and nothing can go outside what I tell you. Everything has to be done in a timely manner and when we are speaking on the phone, we don't speak about what happening just say the word 'done' when your part of the plan is complete."

I look around at them all waiting for them all to understand. "I knew you had it in you. I knew you wouldn't be able to be the sweet, caring Em you always are," Shae says.

"That's where you're wrong. I'm still the sweet, caring Em it's just I'm tired of taking bullshit from mothafuckas that don't give a damn what they put my family through."

"Ok, so what's the plan?" Mya asks.

"First, I need Mya and Shae to run down on bitched named Brandi and Tangy. They are friends with this bitch that can't seem to keep her hands off my husband, and she is running around talking about how I'm ruining her marriage to him. I need for them both to be bound, gagged, and taken to this address." I hand them a piece of paper with an address to a building we were supposed to use as storage at the edge of the city.

"What am I gonna do?" Kacey asks.

"Since this is your friend, you know how to get in touch with her brother. So, I need for you to get him alone and give him this roofie in a drink or something. Then, I want you to call this number and a guy will come and pick him up and take him to the address of the building. Can you do that?"

"Yes, when do we need to do this?"

"Friday. I have some things I need to get taken care of first, but Friday no later than eight o'clock."

"Where can we find the other two women?" Mya ask.

"Their addresses are on the paper under their names. Please don't mess this up ok."

"Will I get to be there when you show up at the building?"

"Yes, you can all be there. Why not?"

I get up to leave when Mya stands and grabs my arm. "Are you sure you want to do this? Once we set this into motion there is no turning back."

"This is happening. If you are getting cold feet then let me know, and I will take care of it myself, but this is what I want to happen," I tell her, looking her square in the eye.

I walk down the sidewalk to my car when a woman starts to walk next to me. "I know you don't know me, but I need to give you a message.' The woman stands right in front of me.

I laugh in her face. "It seems like everybody has a message for me nowadays."

"I don't know what you're talking about," the woman says with pure confusion written all over her face.

"What's your message?" I laugh again.

"I have a friend, and she needs you to leave her man alone. We are all aware you are married to him, but she has something you can't give him."

"And what's that?"

"His baby. She's pregnant right now with his baby, and they need to be a family."

"Let me ask you a question, what do you get out of all this? Being in the mix of some shit that has nothing to do with you." I don't give her a chance to answer and send a punch to her face. She falls into the car, and I blackout repeatedly slamming her head into the window.

"Ma'am ma'am, stop!" a male voice yells to me and a hand grabs me, pulling me away. I look up and see the woman laying on the ground, panting and bleeding. "It's alright, ma'am. Are you ok?"

"Yes, I'm alright." I look around at the people standing around looking with fear and worry.

Mya and Kacey run out of the coffee shop to me. "What the hell just happened?" Mya asks.

"I don't know," I respond.

"This woman was harassing her and she put her on her ass," the man explains, still holding me up by the arm.

"Come on, let's go." Mya grabs me and we step over the woman still laying on the ground. I get into the passenger side of the car, and Mya hops behind the wheel. We pass the police as we drive down the street. "Em, what the fuck? What the fuck did she say?"

"She told me she had a message for me, her friend was pregnant by my husband and they needed to be a family. They needed to be together without me so they can't have what I can't give him." I sob into my hands.

"What? What can't you give him?" she asks, still peeling through the city.

I take a deep breath. "Apparently, I can't give him a baby."

The rest of the car ride is silent as we pull into my driveway and Kacey follows behind us in Mya's car. "Do you want us to come in? We can keep you company for a while."

"No, I just want you all to get ready for Friday. Do what you need to do to make that shit come together." I get out of the car and watch her walk back to her car and leave.

This bitch wants to play games. I'm about to give her the game of a lifetime. She can come for me and mine, but she will learn what consequences are. Death will be the only thing she wishes for. She should have chosen wisely because I'm sure it'll be her last.

Ten

Ember

Today is the day this shit is about to go down and everyone is in position. Markus' little side chick has finally met her match. She wants my spot, but she doesn't realize the dedication, time, and love I have put into this man, and to let him go for someone that just wants to play house is not going to happen. Her arrival at the building has already been given, now I just wait for her friends to join her.

The doorbell rings, and I already know who it is. I open the door to a Mya dressed in all black and Kacey looking just as dumbfounded as ever. "What are y'all doing here? I thought y'all had somewhere to be?" I ask.

"No, we got that shit out of the way last night and they are being taken to the building right now. I just hope you know what you're doing," Kacey wonders.

"Hell yes, she knows what she's doing. I wish I would have done the same when this shit happened to me 'cause Lord knows I went through some shit in that relationship," Mya says.

"Just meet me there at eight. I have to go get Markus and go to dinner."

"We will be there. I don't think he should know we are there though. It's going to make things a little tense," Kacey says.

"Well, it's going to be tense anyway when seeing the bitch he used to fuck on tied to a chair." I laugh. "So are we all still in and ready to handle this shit?"

"Yes."

"Yes," Mya says a little more excited than she was before.

A I wait for Markus to get out of the shower, I sit on the bed in my all white crochet lace long sleeve jumpsuit. "You are so beautiful. Where are you going?" Markus asks, walking out and toweling off.

"You mean where are we going?" I corrected him.

"Ok, then where are we going?" he asks again.

"We are going to dinner and then to have a good time."

"Ok, I like the sound of that."

"I have a question. Do you want to eat first or get your present first?"

"I can wait on the food. Let me see what you have for me."

Going outside to the car, I blindfold him. "Ok you can't see so keep this on." I help him get into the car and start the ten-minute drive to the building. Shae stands outside the building, and I know everyone is already here.

"Why are we stopping? Have we made it to the spot?"

"Yes, we're here." I get out and walk around to let him out of the car. "Ok, careful don't try and walk too fast. The ground is flat, but I don't want you to scuff your shoes. You may need to wear them to a funeral."

"What?"

"Nothing. Just keep walking." The lights in the building are dim, but they get the job done. I push him forward until he's standing in front of his little mistress and take off his blindfold. "Surprise," I say. His eyes go wide as he stares from his mistress to her little friends.

"Em, baby what did you do?" Markus panicked as he looks around the room.

"I'm doing what you can't seem to do. I'm taking care of the problem," I say, gesturing to the four people that sit before us.

"Who is this guy?" he asks.

"Oh that's who was holding me at knifepoint in front of your office that claimed she is his sister, but it turns out he's just another nigga she's fuckin'. So since she's telling you she's pregnant it may be yours and it may not be. But either way, it won't matter here in a few minutes." I walk over to the mistress and snatch off the tape on her mouth. "Now, I have a question for you. Since you set all this shit into motion and sent these mothafuckas after me, what's your name?"

"Em, please, baby don't do this," Markus begs.

"Shut up before you join her. Answer me."

"Lynn," she says.

"Ok, Lynn what makes you think you were going to get away with the shit you pulled on me?"

"I was told that you weren't important and you would be getting a divorce soon."

I look at Markus and the sweat rolling down his face is amusing. "You told Lynn here that we were getting a divorce? Was this before or after I found out you were cheating?"

"Before," Lynn chimed in before Markus could utter a single thing.

I shake my head. "Shae," I call out into the room.

Walking from the far end in the dark, Shae emerges with her bottle of Hennessy. "I got you right here." She walks to me and hands me the bottle and the lighter.

"Since we are playing bald head hoe games, Markus. I want you to pour this on Lynn's head."

"What?"

"So you're slow, now? I want you to pour this on Lynn's head." Lynn lets out a little laugh. "I'm glad you think this is so funny."

Markus takes the bottle from me and drizzles it all over her, drenching her hair in the liquor. "There, you happy?"

"No, I'm not. I want you to set her on fire."

"What the fuck? Hell no. Markus, you better not. I'm pregnant with your baby."

"You're not pregnant. I paid for the abortion remember?"

"Ok, now we have it established that you're not pregnant, shut the fuck up." I take the gun from Shae's waist and point it at Markus. "Now set this bitch on fire."

Mya walks from behind Shae with a bucket in her hand, standing just off from the group awaiting my command. "Baby, I can't do this."

"Oh, you can't? Ok. Don't worry about it." I strike the lighter, setting Lynn in a blaze and watching her burn.

The muffled screams of her friends sound off throughout the room. "Baby, please stop," Markus pleads.

"You're going to beg for this bitch's life, but mine didn't matter when she did all this shit to me? Is that what you're telling me?"

I nod at Mya, and she puts the fire out on Lynn, leaving her hair burned down to the scalp and her clothes partially burned. The smell of her burning flesh makes me want to throw up right in front of them, but I pull it together.

"Em, baby, it's not worth all this. She's not worth all this," Markus says.

"Are you still pleading for this hoe's life? This bitch tried to destroy us, our family and you want to let her get away? I don't think so." I look into the darkness at the other end of the room. "Kacey, is the water boiling yet?"

"Kacey?" Lynn asks, trying to see into the dark.

"Oh that's right you know her, don't you?" The look on her face is priceless as Kacey struts from the dark to bring me the canister of boiling water.

"Kacey, how the fuck are you....why the fuck are you?" Lynn stammers.

"I don't condone the shit you did to her and the fact you knew they were married makes you just as guilty as he is," Kacey says, looking right into her friend's eyes.

"Now the reunion is over. Kacey, I need you to pour that water over Tangy's head here. Can you do that?"

Without a passing word, the water starts to slide down Tangy's face, taking bits of her skin with it. The piercing sound of her screams almost burst my eardrums. I point the gun at the man sitting off to the side.

"What do you want to do with him?" Shae asks.

"Take the tape off his mouth. I have a few questions for him." Shae does her thang and punches him in the face before removing the tape. "Sir, I don't know your name, but when I was told you were fucking this bitch and trying to get in good with her, I knew you had something to do with her being so adamant about trying to trap my husband. What you both thought was she was going to get with him and take him for the businesses and money we have, right? Well, that shit didn't work like planned, huh?" I laughed. I lock eyes with him and shoot him twice in the chest, once in the nuts, and once in the forehead.

"Baby, what are you doing?" Markus asks.

"I told you I'm doing what you couldn't. I'm taking care of your mess."

"Baby it's not too late. We can still walk out of here and be fine."

"Baby we are going to walk out of here without a scratch on us. Now as for Brandi over here. Shae, give this bitch her guts to hold." I watch as Shae cuts deep into her stomach, exposing all her insides.

"Who's next?" I wave the gun around the room at each and last one of them. "No more games." I give the gun to Markus. "I want you to shoot both of them in the head. Right now."

"Baby, I can't do this. I can't shoot them," Markus says.

"It's our family or them. Which is it gonna be?"

"Fine." Markus raises the gun and darkness takes over his whole body. He shoots Lynn in the face until there is nothing left.

"Well since we are out of bullets, I need you to make this interesting for me." I take the knife from Shae and hand it to Markus. "Now don't go easy on her or it's going to be worse for you because remember you're gonna have your turn."

Slowly, he made his way over to the chair that still holds and badly burned Tangy. He flips the knife in his hand, and he doesn't look her in the face before running it across her throat. She struggles against her restraints as she gargles and the blood flows in and out of her throat.

"That's not going to cut it. I need her dead. Now!" I yell at him.

"What the fuck do you want me to do, Em?"

"If I have to tell you what to do then you should call yourself a fuckin' gangsta. Kill this bitch!" I yell again.

He plunges the knife into her chest repeatedly until she stops moving. "Happy?"

"I don't understand what the fuck you are so upset about? You got what you wanted. You don't have to worry about me finding out about your little side bitch and we can still make this marriage work."

"Ok, now what? What are we going to do with them?"

"I already have that taken care of. The movers will be here in about ten minutes to make sure they are properly disposed of. Now, let's go home so I can shower and go to sleep. Baby brain is starting to kick in," I say, walking back to the car.

Markus takes off his shirt and wraps the knife in it and grabs my hand. "I love you, Em, and if this is the only way for you to feel like shit is going to calm down and we can live our lives then fine so be it, but I don't want you to do anything like this again. We are about to have a baby, and we have to think about the safety of our son."

"I understand and as long as no one threatens our house and our family again, then you won't have to worry about this happening again. You have to put your family first and keep people out of it. You are the one that's always talking about keeping people out of our business. Now you take your advice and keep people out of our shit."

I don't know if this is going to last long, but I'm giving him what he wants. I'm giving him all of me, the good, the bad, and the ugly. What he does with it is going to make or break us.

*****

Nine months later

The baby cries into the monitor. "I got him," Markus says, rolling out of bed.

I've always looked forward to this. The man I love taking care of his family. There is nothing no one can do or say to make me walk away from this. The cooing of MJ through the monitor makes my heart smile. They are all I need, and I couldn't have asked for a better life.

To Be Continued

Made in United States
Orlando, FL
03 March 2023

30639419R00075